Praise for David Searls and
Yellow Moon

"Creepy and atmospheric, *Yellow Moon* is full of small-town authenticity. It's like an alternate universe horror version of *The Andy Griffith Show*."

 —Joe R. Lansdale

"Searls is a horror writer who goes for imagination and suspense rather than regurgitated splatter."

 —Ramsey Campbell

"Searls weaves an intricate web of dark intentions and even darker actions with this novel. Well written and well thought out."

 —Shattered Ravings on *Bloodthirst in Babylon*

Look for these titles by
David Searls

Now Available:

Bloodthirst in Babylon
Malevolent

Yellow Moon

David Searls

SAMHAIN
PUBLISHING

Samhain Publishing, Ltd.
11821 Mason Montgomery Rd., 4B
Cincinnati, OH 45249
www.samhainpublishing.com

Yellow Moon
Copyright © 1994 by David Searls
Print ISBN: 978-1-61921-348-7
Digital ISBN: 978-1-61921-302-9

Editing by Don D'Auria
Cover by Scott Carpenter

This book has been previously published.
First Samhain Publishing, Ltd. electronic publication: June 2013
First Samhain Publishing, Ltd. print publication: June 2013

Dedication

To Laura, for eighteen years of great parenting.

Chapter One

May we eat your young?
Pluck the eyes and nibble the tongue?
Ah, those tender ears and noses
Tiny fingers and crunchy toeses
Yes! Yes! Such pitiful mewling cries!
With every bite as the young child dies
And may we eat your old?

No one acid-rained on Carl Thayer's wall without answering to Carl Thayer about it. Especially not some out-of-towner like the one he found doing his private thing so unprivately along the side of Thayer Shell that sunny afternoon about one.

It was Kerri Upshaw, the dyke who ran the town, who'd sent him charging out from under Milt Cory's Pontiac Bonneville and into the blinding early summer or late-spring sun. Carl wasn't a hundred percent sure of the season, since it was supposed to turn over sometime that week or possibly the next or the one just before, but he couldn't recall the specifics.

"Carl, I think we've got a situation here," the town manager had said in that grating way of hers that made Carl want to go for a gun every time he heard it.

He hadn't even looked up at first, figuring she was merely nibbling his ass all over again about that leaky tire of hers, as stubborn in its faults as its leathery owner was in hers. Carl had patched the thing, replaced the valve and stem, done everything but gift-wrap her a new one, but nothing worked.

"Okay, Kerri," he'd mumbled, his round head still buried under the hood of Milt Cory's Pontiac Bonneville with the bad voltage regulator. "But short of proposing and giving you a new set of tires instead of that engagement ring I'm saving up for, I got no new ideas. Soon as you face facts you can only coast so long on worn-out rubber, the sooner you'll see the advantage of buying a new set of my Generals, now on sale for just—"

"Save it, Carl. You've got someone pissing on your wall."

Carl Thayer's head throbbed like a motherfucker the way he bounced it off the hood of Milt Cory's Pontiac Bonneville with the bad voltage regulator, but it certainly added oomph to his fighting mood. Something of a testosterone rush, that skull slam, if there was such a beast.

"Ouch, goddamnit, who the shit—?"

"Shit's not the problem, Carl. Not yet, but wouldn't bet against it."

He was blinking into the spring or summer sun by that time. The sudden white light after three hours in his garage seemed to microwave rational thought and encourage raw instinct.

Rounding the corner in a charge that was already leaking the wind from him like the air from Kerri Upshaw's steel-belted, he crashed into and impressively bounced off of his General Tire display by bay three.

"Side wall," Kerri said, redirecting him. "By the fence."

"Son of a bitch."

The worst part—worse even than the bare-bones fact that someone was spraying his gray brick wall in broad daylight—was that the perpetrator, as he could now plainly see, was no one Carl Thayer had ever laid eyes on. And Carl Thayer knew or at least recognized damned near all eleven-thousand-and-some residents that Cleary, Ohio, claimed.

The stranger wasn't a passing vacationer, either, with a station wagon full of sugared-up kids and a bladder every bit as overloaded as the car. Even the most desperate of that species found time to bribe

Carl for the bathroom key-on-a-stick with murmured promises of fill-ups and plastic sunglass purchases for the entire family.

This was worse.

The stranger grunted, flicked his pecker a few times to be sure and zipped up with a graceless hip swivel to avoid sacrificing original equipment to fastener metal...they don't call 'em teeth for nothing.

Carl had seen this type before. In Cincinnati or Columbus, probably—some big city—but never in Cleary. No sir, no street people on these streets. Folks here owned bathrooms, and even the shiftiest of the shiftless had the decency to leave nature when nature called.

Carl Thayer wrinkled his nose at the salty, acid scent wafting his way along with another whole packet of smells: stale sweat, unbathed skin, unlaundered denim and other things he didn't want to analyze.

The stranger turned his way. The stranger's mouth fell open and stayed that way, apparently undecided between speaking or evacuating lunch. His eyes had once been green. Even from a dozen feet away, Carl could make out the bright red lines running through those abused irises like tiny earthquake faults. The man's hair was dark and clammy, face pale. He was thin, but panther-sleek. He wore jeans that clung like an oil slick, and a cracked vinyl jacket over a lumberjack-plaid shirt. Just for extra measure against the season's harsh seventy-eight degrees, the man had added a down vest.

The outfit confirmed Carl's impression of street types: too much clothing in warm weather, not enough in cold. He'd heard once how drugs played hell on junkie body thermostats. In years, the stranger was somewhere between thirty and fifty, except maybe older or younger.

The man backed up a step.

"Hey," Carl said. He growled the single syllable in a voice that had kept him out of more than one barroom fight. He moved a step forward to match and cancel the other's retreat.

The man turned amazingly fast for someone Carl figured had to be half-dead from liquor or heroin or angel dust, and darted toward the back of the building.

Carl had him now, by God. They were up against the fence back there, just a flimsy little thing creating more of an aesthetic barrier than a physical one between the Paulsens' back yard and Carl's gas station. No matter. Carl Thayer planned to be all over him before the bastard had half a chance to scale it.

The stranger's foot found the middle board. He swung his other leg up. The shoe now on display was one of the brands worn by jocks, drug dealers and teenagers, the only ones who could shell out a hundred bucks for ten flies. But the electrician's tape holding together the sole diminished the status-symbol appeal considerably.

"No one does that on my building," Carl said as he tackled the stranger, tore him off of the wildly swaying little fence and slammed him against the Shell station.

Carl made a thick fist, brought it back and—

—went insane.

In the vast, vast distance he heard what sounded like the ice cream man's merrily tinkling bell, and then...

He hopes it's temporary, this total loss of reason, as the tunnel comes down down down his way and something inside calls out...calling him by name?...and the impossible yellow light...no, not yellow, not any color but closer to yellow than anything else...creeps his way like wet flesh and behind it something else, something long and hard and black. This something else touches Carl Thayer, enters him— his mouth—his soul. Choking. Eyes, frozen immobile eyes, watch Carl while Carl watches the eyes watch; Carl prays that he's safely installed somewhere beyond this scene, where things like this don't really happen. Ever.

One part of him, maybe the remaining sane part, is what's standing back and watching the curious proceedings. This part of Carl Thayer knows that the part that is—was?—Carl Thayer's body, that used to be under Carl Thayer's control, that this part of him is still pinning the stranger to the wall...still aiming that powerful fist... And this sane, abstract part of Carl Thayer—the Mind, maybe—knows that the Body is looking into some kind of hallucination, that the tunnel coming toward him can't possibly be out there, can't hurt him. That the choking sensation as the black thing enters him, pulls itself steadily into his throat, this can't be real. And the eyes, the watching eyes from high above him don't count. Don't exist.

Can't exist.

He gags.

"Carl? *Carl.*"

He blinked. Gradually recognized the rock-gargling voice that could belong to only one woman here on God's favorite planet.

Carl ripped his hands away from the foul-odored stranger and stumbled backward until his knees gave out and his ass found the weedy, cracked pavement. His breath rushed from his fiery lungs as if suddenly unstopped. The tunnel and the eyes disappeared like the illusion they had been.

Carl Thayer, Mind and Body, was back in Cleary, Ohio. His throat itched, raw. Kerri Upshaw told him to take it easy as he jumped back to his feet.

The grimy man before him shielded his face with two shaking arms. There was certainly fear in that face, but something else as well. Something more important than fear momentarily lit the stranger's used-up green eyes. "This's it," he mumbled. "Shit yes, it's here now. The bad dream of all time, it's here now. Can't be worse now than it was. All the bad dreams and the yellow moon and the gods of the drains. Oh, yeah, I been seeing for a long time what you be seeing now. Enjoy it, motherfucker." He cackled.

Least that seemed to be the general tone of the message, the stranger's voice rattling loosely past the places in his mouth where teeth once dwelt. "Jesus coming in the bad dreams. Think it's Jesus, hope it's Jesus in the bad dreams with the gods of the drains."

"You'll need Jesus if we catch you hosing any more of our buildings." Kerri stood by the General Tire display, arms out like on safety patrol. Her eyes looked tired, but that was the expression she

11

assumed during her most dangerous moods. Watch out for those sleepy eyelids of hers. Her stork legs, brown and tight in one of the season's first pair of shorts, held up a hard, jutting body. One lesbo you just didn't fuck with, if anyone were to ask Carl Thayer's opinion.

The stranger turned and practically pole-vaulted that back fence without a pole.

"Stop him," Carl croaked, half-surprised that he had any voice left at all.

"Oh, sure thing," Kerri grunted. "And I'm Arnold Schwarzenegger."

"Closer to it than most of us." Carl Thayer sniffed his hands. They smelled like they felt, diseased by contact with the stranger. Wasn't that one of the ways to catch AIDS? Hug a drug addict? Now there was something, to die like a homosexual—a married man of fifty-four—and have the entire town spreading vicious lies.

So now the stranger had pissed on his wall, knocked him on his ass *and* given him a fatal gay junkie disease.

Turning into some kind of Saturday afternoon, it was.

Chapter Two

"Hey, Tom, what the hell you doing here?"

"Nothing. Checking things out, that's all." To Tom Luckinbill's ears, his own response sounded too quick, too pat, too defensive.

Officer Jeff Smith looked up from the front desk, smiled, shook his head sadly. The dispatch radio crackled, ignored, in the background. "Knew you couldn't stay away. Now Joanie's going to sue your ass for sole custody and you'll never see your little chillen again."

Tom grunted to show he was taking the younger man's comment like the joke it was supposed to be. That it wasn't feeding his moderate paranoia on that same subject.

"Kidding," Jeff said, just setting the record straight.

Tom shrugged. "They're twelve and fourteen." He stopped to consider. He certainly had their approximate ages, but he could be off by a birthday or two. God, he hoped he hadn't missed a birthday. "They don't want to spend every weekend moment with the old man. They need room to breathe." Whatever that meant.

"Yeah," Jeff said agreeably.

Tom ordered his tongue to plead the Fifth. He let his eyes roam only to escape his officer's gently taunting grin. The police station looked cheerfully abandoned. It had been someone's idea to paint the place white, lighten it up, make those tacky public service posters thumb-tacked everywhere really stand out. What it actually accomplished, all that crisp, bright airiness, was to make the place look too big, too desolate.

"Anyone here?" Tom knew he was only imagining that his voice was echoing back at him.

Jeff braced himself with both elbows on the high counter separating the two of them. "Just you and me, boss. Glenn Leighton's old man bailed him out couple hours ago, same's he does about every other Saturday morning after sonny's had himself too much fun at The Bluegrass."

Tom grunted again, shook his head and turned to walk away.

"Oh, nearly forgot our dangerous felon in cell six," Jeff added, calling him back. "Urinated on Carl Thayer's Shell station. Street type, no ID and no comment. Nothing that makes sense to us mere human beings, anyway. Mark brought him in after the alleged victim called in a description. Carl's asking for the electric chair, of course, but I thought we could show some of our small-town compassion and merely castrate the poor bastard."

"If you mean Carl, it's fine with me."

Jeff's face pinkened with appreciation. The blush was how Tom Luckinbill always knew when he'd matched the quick wit of his twenty-four-year-old deputy.

"Did our mystery guest offer any resistance?" Tom asked.

"Guess he ran, but pooped out quick—pardon the continuing bathroom theme here. He was fine once Mark caught up and has been a helluva lot easier to deal with than Glenn Leighton. Or Carl Thayer, for that matter."

"He's in back?"

"The stranger? Oh, yeah. In the cell farthest from the door."

"Meaning...?"

"He doesn't smell too good. Maybe we ought to just let Carl take him out back and shoot him."

The front door slammed open at that exact moment and Carl Thayer himself shoved into the whitewashed lobby of the lonely police station.

"I hear you got my man," Carl Thayer said, sounding like Marshal Dillon anticipating his prisoner's extradition.

Tom hoped the service station owner hadn't heard Jeff's last comment; it might get his hopes up.

"Yeah, we got him," Jeff said, putting on his best lawman drawl.

"Good thing." Carl actually rubbed his palms together. "Can I see him?"

The two cops exchanged glances. The balding younger one started to blush once again with restrained humor.

Tom cleared his throat. "Well, Carl, it's not like we've found this guy's poster on the post office wall or anything."

"I think he's dangerous," Carl roared. "Diseased, at the very least. I should ID the perpetrator, shouldn't I? Seeing that he did assault me with no witnesses but Kerri Upshaw, who hates my guts for whatever reason and probably wouldn't be a reliable witness anyway."

Tom studied the silence that followed. Shrugged. "Tell me, Carl. Why didn't I spend the afternoon with my boys like I honestly intended?"

Carl's reply was a defensive stare: somehow, he seemed to figure, he had to be the butt of the joke. The problem was catching the punch line.

"Forget it," Tom said. "Jeff, take him back, huh? Let him ID the perpetrator, whatever."

Jeff nodded solemnly. "The *pissatrator*, I suppose it would be. But be careful, Mr. Thayer. We haven't checked his anal cavity for concealed weapons yet. You care to help us out?"

Carl glared; Tom smiled, a facial twitch too quick and impermanent to be held against him. He grabbed the loose stack of freshly delivered mail that looked to be his, and headed back to the closet he called an office. He plopped behind his desk, where yesterday's newspaper mingled with yesterday's cigarette ash and the remaining contents of yesterday's Sprite can. He gently nudged a clear space with a thick forearm—softly brushing the accumulation aside seemed somehow less disorganized than a more forceful sweep—and released the unopened pile of trade magazines and circulars over the reclaimed territory. Then he examined the stiff sleeve of that same forearm, carefully brushing away an imaginary smudge of ash from otherwise spotless uniform blues.

Tom Luckinbill had nearly convinced himself that his lack of organization was the reason Joanie had left him. She'd called him a fraud once, said he'd deceived her with his spit-shine personal image, then pressed her nose to the unkempt reality of his existence only when it had been too late for her to back out.

Or so she'd thought at the time.

He stared at the phone, let his mind run through a dozen numerical combinations before it latched on to his home number.

No, they were probably out anyway. Of course, he could leave a message, tell them he was on his way home in case they got back before he did.

Back from where? They'd mentioned their plans for the day at breakfast, hadn't they? Or had that been yesterday morning they'd all eaten together?

Anyway, he'd make it up, take them out for burgers or toss a Frisbee or hang out with them at the Mundy Street Pool, whatever it was Greg and Tony did these days. Tom could imagine how tough it might be prying them back out of Columbus any time soon if Joanie found out how little time they'd spent with the old man this time around.

He wanted them back, didn't he?

Of course he did. They were his kids, and it wasn't like anyone else was monopolizing his attention these days.

"Ready for this?"

Tom jumped, guilty at being caught doing nothing behind that overworked-looking desktop.

Jeff was leaning on his doorjamb, eyes aglitter at someone's expense.

The police chief shook his head. "Probably not."

Now that his thoughts were refocused, he could hear Carl Thayer braying as he approached the doorway.

"Ain't funny, Tom, despite what your Jeff here thinks. I'm telling you, we all live in a small town and pay pretty good property taxes so we don't have to put up with this horseshit."

"Easy, Carl, easy." Tom ran both hands through his dark hair. "What particular horseshit are we talking about, Jeff?"

Officer Smith wet his lips, took a deep breath and started slowly, as if what he had to say came difficult. But his bright eyes couldn't match the careful level of concern in his voice. "Carl says the man we got locked up isn't the one who knocked him down this afternoon. He thinks that—"

"No one knocked you down this afternoon, Carl. You slipped and fell."

All three men jumped as town manager Kerri Upshaw filled the doorway, pushing the occupancy level of the tiny office well beyond the pain threshold of the average claustrophobic. She took turns glaring at each of the other three, taking her time with Officer Smith.

"So if we're all socializing in here," she asked, "who's minding the phones and dispatch radio?"

Jeff blushed, his eyes no longer glittering. "I am, ma'am."

"Not from in here, you're not. Things are squawking out there, son. I'd get on it."

Jeff fled to the lobby.

"Think he's scared of me, Tom?"

Tom Luckinbill might have seen the faintest glint of amusement in the woman's smudgy eyes. It was a remote possibility, anyway. He nodded. "I'm damned sure of it, Kerri."

"Good." Now she turned her attention to the police chief's other visitor. "I thought I'd drop by, see that Carl got his story straight when he petitioned you for a rope and a willow tree. And by the way, Carl, you've got no permit for beating up folks who mistake your wall for the men's room. You got what was coming to you, but he wasn't the one did it. You fell trying to tackle that fellow, don't tell me you didn't."

Carl danced the kind of flailing two-step that baseball managers invented to indicate differences of opinion with the umpiring crew. "I

17

knew you'd say something like that, Kerri, but I'm telling you—there's something weird about that guy. If you'd have touched him, you'd have known it, too. Course," he added, voice dropping real low, "I forgot how repugnant the idea of touching a man must be to you."

"You didn't seem to mind the idea of close personal contact with this fellow, Carl."

Carl sputtered, "If you're saying—"

"Stop the bickering, you two," Tom ordered. "What do you mean, Carl? What happened when you touched him?"

"Doesn't matter," Kerri said. "We're not all singing from the same hymnal anyway. I hear someone say you got the wrong one locked up back there?"

Carl stuck his hands on his hips, offering his best scowl to whoever wanted it. "Yeah, there's two of them now. What do you have to say about that, Tom?"

"Not just two."

All three stared at the young cop who'd returned to the chief's crowded office.

Tom wanted details.

"First Darlene Garrett spots a raggedy man digging through the garbage bin behind the Harvest House. Next thing I hear is how Steve and Vern stopped three more of them shuffling down Bridge Street about a mile off of Route 35. They're asking right now whether or not they should bring 'em in on a ten thirty-nine."

"Prowlers," Tom explained to his frowning town manager. He saw the last wisps of his halfhearted Saturday-afternoon-with-the-boys fantasy fading fast, like so many before. "They doing anything, Jeff? Causing any trouble?"

"Just walking. Jaywalking, probably. Touching themselves in public. Molesting French poodles...whatever you want the citation to read."

Tom shook his head. "Leave them alone."

"What about the one Jay Pitts saw panhandling outside his hardware store?"

"Jesus, that's right by my place," Carl bellowed. "You know what fresh piss smells like on a hot afternoon?"

"Where are they all coming from?" Kerri asked, her tough face holding up a confused frown.

That, Tom thought, *is the million-dollar question.*

Chapter Three

Ben Crocker was in his bedroom welcoming the new summer with Trevor Kincaid, Danny Young and Skippy Crenshaw. Their legs, too thin and pale, looked unnatural in the season's virgin pairs of baggy shorts. It was the first of twelve straight school-less Saturdays, and the four eleven-year-olds were enjoying nothing more than the organized planning of the sunny times that stretched lazily ahead.

"*This* summer I'm learning to swim," Skippy was promising for what had to be the third straight June.

"Bullshit," answered Danny, who was sturdier and darker than pale, frail Skippy, but his best friend and toughest critic. "You wear a life jacket in the shower."

Three youngsters howled at the expense of the fourth, who heaved a handy shoe at his chief tormentor.

"What about you, Trevor?" Ben asked.

"Mm?"

"What are you going to do this summer?"

Trevor was draped belly-down over the bed, rifling through Ben's baseball card collection. Occasionally, he'd set one aside that seemed to interest him mildly, one that might make him part with his third-year Canseco Upper Deck if the deal was right. Trevor shrugged. He was the tallest of Ben's friends, a quiet boy whose words carried more weight than most. "My folks are sending me to wildlife camp in August, but—"

"Oh, God," Danny screamed in cruel delight. "Wildlife camp. And we thought Skippy was weird."

"Shut up, Danny," Ben ordered. "My dad's downstairs."

"Sorry, but that's just like Trevor. He'll spend half the summer in camp to learn about stuff and half in the library."

"Yeah," Skippy said. "And the other half watching the Discovery Channel."

"You really got your fractions down, Skippy," Trevor said.

Skippy and Danny glanced at each other, then burst into peals of laughter. Ben wasn't sure either of them understood the joke, but that didn't affect their reaction.

"Shut up," Ben repeated. "I told you...my dad."

"We don't want to piss off the mayor," Danny said with obvious sarcasm. "Let's go play ball."

"Just the four of us?" Ben asked, screwing his round face up.

Danny shook his head. "Forgot to mention, Greg and Tony are in town. I saw them playing catch in the park on my way over here."

Inwardly, Ben winced. At fourteen and thirteen, Greg and Tony were taller, wider, stronger and faster than anyone else Ben hung out with. His one goal in life was to be as cool as either Luckinbill brother, but that wasn't going to happen if he was attached at the hips to squirrel bait like Skippy and Danny.

"We don't have to go," Skippy was saying, evidently catching the doubt in Ben's eye.

Ben glanced at Trevor, his best friend. The other boy barely shrugged, indicating a willingness to be swayed either way. Although Trevor was a brain, there was such a lack of dependence on the attitudes of others that it let him escape the torments brought on so many others with similar thirsts for knowledge. The boys in town seemed to respect Trevor's quiet self-assurance, or merely to know that derision would have no effect, so why waste a good laugh?

Ben nodded. "Let's go play ball."

"Wait, guys," Skippy said. His face looked uncustomarily serious. Ben waited for the bad joke that was sure to follow, but all he heard was, "We could go some other time."

"What?" Danny screeched, his voice reaching a decibel level guaranteed to draw the unwanted attention of an annoyed parent or two. "Skippy, how come you're so chickenshit?"

"I'm not chickenshit," the boy replied from his crouching position on the floor. He was making too much eye contact with the others, as far as Ben was concerned. A dead giveaway, if you knew Skippy well. "Just...I don't know. Maybe we could do something else, that's all."

Trevor let his slim body slither from the bed. He fell effortlessly into a squatting position on the floor next to Skippy and stared him down. "Come on, what is it?" he asked quietly.

Skippy fired up a smile, but it didn't seem to fit his jumpy eyes. Danny and Ben hunched next to Trevor, triple-teaming the suddenly uncommunicative one.

"Nothing, nothing," Skippy mumbled. "Just...I kind of had a dream."

"How can you 'kind of have a dream'?" Ben wanted to know.

"What was it about?" Trevor asked.

"I'm not really sure."

"Great." Danny snickered.

Trevor shushed him with a distracted wave of his hand. "Tell us."

Skippy stared at Ben's Reds pennant over his headboard. At least that seemed to be what was holding his interest. When Skippy spoke, his voice sounded almost eager to share the experience. "We were playing ball in my dream, which is why, you know, I'm kind of nervous. But not scared. Just nervous. A bunch of us, we were playing, and this hole opened up. No." Skippy shoved a fist toward his mouth as if to stuff back his imprecise memory. "Not a hole. More like a tunnel or... something. Whatever."

Danny rolled his eyes. "And," he prompted impatiently.

"That's it, really. Or all I remember. It was just scary, that's all. Scary 'cuz something wanted us to go in. Or wanted to come out. I forget which."

"So what happened?" Trevor asked.

22

Skippy shook his head slowly. "It was all fuzzy, my dream, not making sense most of the time, but scary. Greg and Tony were there too, I think. So when Danny said let's play baseball with the Luckinbills, well…"

Ben's stomach tingled, but he laughed with Danny. Trevor stared. "Cool," he said quietly. "You ever had dreams like this before?"

Skippy frowned in concentration, then shook his head. "Just last night."

Trevor seemed to consider this for seconds longer before dismissing it with a shrug.

"Come on," Danny ordered. "Let's play ball and forget this Twilight Dream Zone crap."

Skippy said, "You guys go ahead. I'm not—"

"Yes you are, you little yellow-belly," Danny screeched.

"Quiet," Ben hissed. "If you two are going to act like squirrels, we'll let Greg and Tony beat the shit out of you." As if he and Trevor could stop them anyway. "Now let's get going."

"Oh, I'm going to have tons of fun," Skippy grumbled as the four filed noisily down the stairs of the Crocker home.

Chapter Four

"For chrissake," Thad Crocker said of the pipe-rattling din just beyond the basement's low ceiling.

"The kids," Megan explained. "Sounds worse because we're standing under the stairs."

Thad looked up. He was stalling, not really all that interested in or irritated by the sudden commotion. "We're gonna find ourselves *literally* under the stairs one of these days when Ben and his friends get bigger," he complained, his voice competing with the seismic rumble of overhead footfalls.

His wife chuckled. "The least of our problems once Ben and Jessie hit the teenage years."

"Oh, joy," Thad replied glumly.

The next harsh sound was of the screen door being flung open, followed by the flat boom of the oak front door slamming shut, rearranging dust particles in the unfinished basement.

"Certain things we can always depend on," Thad said. "Seeing as how we've got no air conditioning, they're very careful to close the door behind them in the summertime. Wait till the coldest day on record, and it's a different story."

Megan swatted him playfully. "You're a grouch. You're getting old before your time. And you're stalling."

Thad looked down, then backed up a half step. The gray, foamy water had crawled another couple inches his way since his last distraction. It seemed to move only when left unobserved. "Reminds me of *The Blob*," he muttered.

"Steve McQueen's dead, and I don't think he ever did make house calls, so you'll have to figure this one out for yourself."

"How come no matter how liberated you women become, you always come to a man for your plumbing needs?"

"Because, in this case, the man's a plumbing wholesaler."

"Community property. You own half of everything that's mine."

"Everything but genetic instinct. I just married into this hotbed of plumbing knowledge."

"I sell the stuff. Don't use it. That was my dad and granddad's department."

Megan Crocker smiled. "The politician in you won't let you lose an argument. So you win: I should know as much about drain opening as you do, but I don't. So when do you think you'll be finished?" She smiled sweetly. "I'll be upstairs."

Actually, the problem wasn't nearly as difficult as he'd made it out to be. Just messy. The whole family had the nasty habit of dumping dirty clothes on the basement floor right in front of the washer so that an adventurous sock or undergarment could worm its way into the nearby floor drain. But as experienced as Thad was at rectifying this particular problem, he'd never gotten used to the squish factor.

He took off his canvas shoes and stepped delicately forward, making a face as the cold, slimy water licked his naked feet: the squish factor. "Jesus," he muttered.

The drain was the center of the storm, but he had to slog through unseen folds of waterlogged clothing to get to it. He gasped every time submerged cotton bumped his bare feet like drowned rats.

The basement's clutter reminded him of the condition of their attic or his garage workroom. All three were examples of those private places where everyone but the most anal retentive let loose their innermost desire to disarrange, to abominate. That's how he excused the unsorted piles of laundry, the upturned boxes, abandoned coffee cans and kitchen appliances, the gutted dryer. From the pipe-decorated ceiling, the single fluorescent tube still fluttering hundreds of hours past usefulness did little more than add depth and motion to the daylight-defeating shadows. The basement looked a good forty years older than the rest of the newish Tudor.

At the center of the sudsy flood, Thad reached down quickly—before he could think about it—and grabbed and pulled away heavy loads of soaked underwear, T-shirts and jeans. They splatted onto dry concrete like baby flood victims. Thad's hand skipped through the chilly water until it found the drain. He grabbed the waterlogged fabric which was caught just a few inches below water level, and tugged.

The gray water tried to suck back the wet material, but Thad outmuscled it, creating a small, soapy whirlpool that replaced his hand and the nearly colorless piece of clothing it held.

Thad groaned. "Aw, look at this," he told no one. It was his favorite shirt. Or, if he'd never thought of the once boldly colored Sea World T-shirt in such glowing terms in the past, he did now as he eulogized it. He balled it up, squeezed out at least a few pounds of water and—

Thad.

He froze. Listened.

"Megan?" he called quietly. "That you?"

Silence.

He didn't think so. It hadn't sounded like his wife's voice. Hadn't sounded like it was coming from the top of the stairs, either.

Thad.

He stood. Backed away. Stared into the black hole of the washing machine drain, still gurgling with rinse water.

He smiled the kind of encouraging smile kids try on while surrendering bad report cards. Weird. Like he heard a voice from the drain. Right.

And more than just the voice. He'd heard something underneath it, and even more distant. A gentle, nostalgic sound that almost reminded him of the bored occasion or two when he'd picked up a delicate knickknack in a china shop, not knowing or caring what to expect, and had been subjected to the soft, teasing lilt of frail music. Music box music.

No...not quite. Similar, but now other memories stirred. Hot, lazy, sticky summer afternoons of long ago, interrupted by...

The ice cream man.

The ice cream man in his basement drain.

Thad jumped as the phone shrilled from the post behind him, but his eyes didn't leave his concrete floor.

He took a very slow step forward and knelt down. Every muscle tensed like the time he'd tried cornering the bat in Ben's room with a bedsheet.

No voice. No music. Just a black drain still partially constipated with errant laundry.

Following the second ring, Thad heard his wife's quick footfalls overhead as she rushed to grab it before the answering machine kicked in.

He bent over the man-made hole in his concrete floor, stared in, looking and feeling as inept as a dog at a rabbit warren.

Something moved.

Thad's lower stomach tightened, but he forced himself to hold his ground.

"Thad?"

He jumped, yelped, fell and rolled backwards until his head crashed into a junk end table, sending a plastic cooler and broken ice cream maker crashing to the hard floor.

"Thad, what's going on? Tom Luckinbill's on the phone. Sounds like you're going to have to play mayor this afternoon."

Thad rose to his knees. "Got it," he said, voice no more than a croak. He picked up the receiver and got a hurried and very incomplete introduction to Cleary's most unique crisis ever. In a minute he would forget about the voice he couldn't have possibly heard in the first place.

Chapter Five

Mayor Thad Crocker hadn't known what to expect when he strolled into the Cleary police station at a few minutes past five that afternoon. The formidable look on Chief Luckinbill's face didn't help ease his mind any, not even knowing that the other man's frown was as natural as his kettle-black hair and hard, flat belly. It wasn't directed at Thad personally, that frown. Just seemed that way.

The cop stared Thad down with those dark eyes of his before chopping the air with a single downward jerk of his head. "Thanks for coming."

Thad took a deep breath. "What is it, Tom? On the phone you sounded kind of serious."

Thad had been given about four minutes to think about the problem as he drove from his comfortable home on Merryside to the downtown police station. One end of town to the other. According to what Thad had learned by phone, there was some kind of situation developing with street people, but things couldn't be all that bad.

Thad had spotted a few shabby strangers on the drive down, but only because he'd been watching for them. Not one of them had looked all that dangerous, really. Not bad enough to justify the police chief's concern.

At least his drive-by scrutiny had given Thad an opportunity to study his hometown, and he wasn't proud of what he was forced to see. He tried to recall what had happened to the family-owned diners and the lumberyards and Bailey's watch repair shop and the overweight realtor (Croston? Crossley?) who'd always sponsored the Fourth of July municipal picnic. How about Rolando Sons, the tiny bakery famous enough to have been written up in newspapers as far away as Cleveland? They had all disappeared, slipped away in the night. More recently, both of the town's mom-and-pop video stores had been blitzkrieged by an international corporation armed with the brash boast of ten thousand movies each and every day of the year, Christmas most definitely included.

At some unobserved point, the international fast-food palaces and chain discount stores and boutique shopping malls had planted themselves on Bridge Street and on Cleary Center and out on Highway 35, leaving Thad Crocker's town looking exactly like every other town of its size in America. Eleven thousand unique citizens had all lost control together, and let outsiders reshape the face of the one thing that belonged to them: the town itself.

Now Thad noticed two things, both of which could spell trouble. First, the telephones in the small police station were ringing off the hooks. And second, he could hear the raw, scraping voice of town manager Kerri Upshaw jawing into a phone next to the young officer with the long face and thin scalp: Warren and Dixie Smith's kid, Jim or Jeff or something.

Chief Luckinbill noticed where Thad's attention had wandered. He nodded. "Serious enough to attract Kerri," he said.

In a flat tone, Thad replied, "That doesn't necessarily mean anything. I've seen our Ms. Upshaw chase her share of ambulances."

As the part-time mayor, Thad was the small town's Prince Charles: he made unimportant speeches and shook hands while the council-appointed town manager got to play Maggie Thatcher on a full-time basis to get the real work done. She handled things well enough, but Thad couldn't help reminiscing about past generations of Crocker mayors who had ruled without such interference. He was usually able to mask his chronic, low-level resentment, but there were a handful of occasions when his true feelings slipped out.

Tom might have displayed slight amusement at Thad's comment concerning the town manager, but the rarely observed phenomenon of a smile was repealed before it could be verified. The chief turned away and said, "Jeff, what's the story so far?"

The young cop cradled his phone on a shoulder. "Sheriff Gattis says he can send out a county car every once in a while, but unless something actually happens there's not much else he can do."

"Jerk," Tom said mildly.

Jeff paused, as if considering the possibility that his boss was addressing him. He shrugged, nodded and continued. "I've talked to lots of folks...bureaucrats...in Columbus, but it's after-hours now, weekend and all. State Highway Patrol will give us top priority if anyone gets violent, but right now—"

"What the hell's going on?" Thad demanded. He wasn't hearing the kind of words a part-time mayor appreciates: *Highway Patrol...top priority...violent...* All he knew—or wanted to know—was that they had a couple vagrants hanging around town. Not too many minutes before, he'd been smugly pleased at being called in to head up the town's crisis management team, and had even imagined pulling rank on Kerri—a fantasy if ever there was one—but now this...

Highway Patrol...top priority...violent...

He zoomed in on Kerri's phone voice, actually hearing what she was saying for the first time.

"Yes, yes, we're aware of the situation, Mrs. Pershing, and we're giving it our full attention. If any of those men does anything besides just walk around, be sure to tell us and we'll take care of it. In the meantime..."

Thad thought again about one of the characters he'd noticed on his way in. The man had certainly looked suspicious by Cleary standards, with his tattered red shoes and rumpled appearance. Up close, Thad knew, the stranger's face would be broken-veined and red as anger. Red as his rotting shoes, and as mutilated as the faces of the villains in any number of Thad's late-night, movie-induced nightmares as a boy.

And for just a moment back there in his car he'd wondered what sort of dreams could pull that ravaged stranger out of his own troubled sleep. Did the man's nightmares contain human monsters with diseased, mirror-image faces of his own? Or was he haunted by the mundane horrors of missed meals, frozen nights and dangerous streets?

"Tell me about it," Thad said to his police chief. "What's happening here?"

Tom Luckinbill was older, stockier, not as tall as the young mayor. He beckoned with a sharp twitch of his head. "Let's talk in my office."

Even at the age of thirty-six it was difficult stepping into Chief Luckinbill's office or, for that matter, having any contact with the lawman. Thad had frequently wondered, especially during his election campaign, whether Tom remembered him as the spoiled punk he'd been, the rich kid the cop had stopped twice for underage drinking-and-driving offenses. Thad had half-suspected that his earlier reputation and silver-spoon upbringing had been the reason Tom had publicly backed his mayoral opposition, Billy Braddox, one of the town's councilmen since sometime shortly after the dawn of time.

Although Thad and the police officer would never be called friends—the twelve-year age difference and dissimilar backgrounds made that unlikely—they worked well together. Thad couldn't remember a single time when he felt he didn't have the full cooperation of the head cop who'd crashed his parties during his misdemeanor-prone teens and stymied his election campaign with his blunt honesty years later.

"Let me clear some of this stuff away," Tom mumbled. He looked honestly embarrassed—as he should be, Thad thought—at the catastrophic office mess. Files, reports and trade journals mingled with Burger King lunch wrappers in a way that seemed designed to challenge fire or pestilence. Different story entirely than Thad's own very covert basement-attic-garage shabbiness.

Thad couldn't help looking from the man to the office; from spit and shine to, well, just plain spit.

When a path to a chair was cleared, Tom impatiently waited for his guest to claim it. "Street types," he said without preamble. "They've been seen since late this morning. Not doing anything beyond irritating the citizenry, but in record numbers."

Thad let that sink in, angling into the ramifications from a politician's point of view. His conclusions: there goes the town; there goes the job. "Any idea where they come from?"

"Not much. We've got a few in holding cells for minor offenses, but on the rare occasions when they can give us a home address, it's likely to be Venus. The ones that drove in, we got license plates. Those we're tracking as far away as New York, Pittsburgh, West Virginia. The rest, if they haven't done anything illegal, we don't dare disturb their precious civil rights by questioning them." Tom rolled his eyes. "ACLU. You know how it is."

Thad stared at the floor, then the ceiling. If he was looking for inspiration, he found none. "Are they together?"

Tom rubbed his face. "Don't appear to be, but I'm not sure they're sure. It's like it's just one huge, goofy coincidence they're all showing up in Cleary, Ohio, at the same time. Jeff and Kerri are checking with as many government agencies as they can find open. You know, see if there's been any mass breakouts anywhere, state hospitals and such. Still wouldn't explain why they're all winding up here, but it'd be a start."

"What have you come up with so far?"

Tom slapped his cluttered desktop with a large, tanned hand. "Nothing. Something like this should have made the news. We should have heard about a breakout on the radio or TV. Hell, the nearest psycho ward isn't just down the road, you know. These people have been traveling a while."

Thad stood. He wanted to pace, but the room's dimensions and clutter forbade it. Feeling dumb just standing there, he resumed a sitting position. "What else do they have in common, these...people?"

"Mostly male, mostly white, but a few haggard-looking women and a couple blacks. Course those are the ones *really* riling the good townfolk, the colored guys."

Thad saw his next election going down the drain, then wondered why he really cared about losing his part-time job. All it did was keep his mind off the wholesale plumbing business for a few hours a week.

But of course he had the answer all along. He couldn't lose the job his old man had passed down to him after serving four of his own terms and retiring to Florida. The office was as much a Crocker family tradition as the business.

He certainly couldn't think of a more logical reason for holding on to his thankless position at the moment.

"Where are they now?" he asked.

Tom rubbed his eyes. "Everywhere. They're loose, if that's what you mean. Justine Pope's on vacation— doesn't it figure?—so I can't get a legal opinion. I wanted to chance it and haul them off the streets without our law director's say in the matter, but Kerri called an attorney friend of hers in Columbus. He said their lawyers would have our balls if we even tried. So I've got Pete and Mark and even my off-duty people in squad cars just waiting for suspicious characters to fart within a hundred yards of a church."

Thad stood up again. He couldn't bear another moment in that littered little office, especially since he could see the police chief fumbling in his crisp shirt pocket for a cigarette. He removed himself to the open doorway.

Tom smiled with his dark eyes. "If you can keep your loyal electorate from lynching any of our guests at least through the weekend, I think I can come up with some answers Monday morning. There's gotta be a government agency that'll help us. Which agency, I don't know yet. But we'll find out once Columbus reopens for business."

Thad sighed. "Keep me posted."

That sounded like a movie line, he thought as he walked back to the station's tidy, whitewashed lobby. *Keep me posted.* Thad fervently hoped there wasn't going to be a reason for further communication until Monday.

Chapter Six

There are countless variations of the game of baseball, most of them spur-of-the-moment inventions without written rules or consistency. You can mandate speed of pitches or handicap scores. The pitcher might also play first. Four outfielders or one. You can play with a softball but retain baseball rules—or with a baseball, using softball rules. And there's no reason that game equipment can't consist of a tennis ball, waffle ball, golf ball or pebble.

It's not just the underprivileged who make these rules and equipment substitutions. Bored descendants of the middle class can be just as inventive.

The six boys in Arthur Waylock Memorial Park played each and every variation of America's pastime that came to mind. The most equitable team breakdown featured the older, huskier Greg and Tony against everyone else, with Skippy tossed in to cover very deep outfield. Their game broke up at least a half-dozen times, but the limits of small-town amusement kept drawing them back to their crude diamond.

Ben and Trevor exchanged embarrassed glances at each of their immature friends' antics: Skippy's ridiculously inaccurate Bart Simpson imitations and Danny's high-pitched "It's not fair, do it over!" every time the other team got a hit. Ben had wanted to be like the Luckinbill brothers for as long as he could remember, but wasn't going to get that way by hanging out with the Odd Couple.

The Luckinbills were more like twins than brothers a year and a half apart in age. You had to really look to see that fourteen-year-old Greg was heavier, more solidly built. Tony was perhaps a hair's breadth taller than his older brother, but slim, and with the athletic grace of a safari animal. Both were dark-haired and swarthy, like their folks. Neither spoke much, but possessed a paradoxical sense of leadership without self-assurance, much like their father. It left them looking and acting serious to the point of grumpiness, like they knew they were to be followed, but remained ill at ease with the sociological fact of the matter.

"I say we call it quits," Skippy screamed from the outfield depths. "It's gonna be dark soon."

Ben rolled his eyes at Trevor, who was kneeling at their homemade "on deck" circle. Danny snickered for some unfathomable reason.

"Stay there, Crenshaw," Greg growled in that deep, almost adult voice of his. "Two more outs." He was pitching, while his brother roved the infield.

"Dark's when it's the most fun," Tony added, barely loud enough to be heard.

Darkball was another variation of the old sport. A dusk game, it involved frantic mental calculations of the missile's trajectory and speed from the sound it made coming off the bat. A correct computation and a lot of luck could result in a catch. A misjudgment, however, scored only a lumpy forehead or purple eye.

"Aw, shit, you guys," Skippy whined. "Last time we played in the dark I got...well, it hurt like hell."

Danny giggled. "Yeah, he got his nuts creamed. Dincha, Skippy?"

"Just shut up, okay," Ben muttered. "Both of you. Stand in, Trevor, and let's get this game over with."

Greg's pitch came in hard and low, but Trevor hit it. The tallest of the four friends, Trevor was the best athlete as well as the smartest.

The ball lifted nicely. Ben watched it arc into the air, somehow catching and throwing back the rays from the lowering sun. Greg, Tony, Danny and even Trevor watched the still upwardly projecting missile.

The trouble was, Skippy was watching it too.

35

"Catch it, Crenshaw," Greg shouted, the husky command to his voice jolting the lone outfielder into action.

Tony shook his head from deep second base. "Never get to it," he predicted with a grunt.

Trevor trotted to first, then second.

Skippy Crenshaw, all twig limbs and Adam's apple, backpedalled for all he was worth: not much, the other boys would have agreed, if value is measured in athletic skills.

Trevor rounded second, tagged third.

Skippy stumbled back and back and back as the ball began its final plunge. He optimistically stabbed at it with his glove, though glove and fielder both trailed the ball by twenty feet as it hit mother earth and rolled into the line of trees that defined home-run country.

"Way to go, asswipe," Danny chortled.

Skippy disappeared into the gathering shadows.

They waited.

For some indistinct reason, Danny began to trot the bases backwards, as if taking credit for Trevor's hit.

Ben twitched his nose, smelling something very wrong. Trevor nudged him and nodded toward the Luckinbills. They were leaning against the oak tree that served as a backstop, lit cigarettes dangling from their lips, and looking for all the world like a couple of hard hats on work break. Ben evaded eye contact when Greg looked his way. He didn't want to be offered one. Somehow he just knew his mom would smell tobacco on him when he was still a block away. She was like that.

Trevor faked an unconcerned yawn, but Ben could see that his best friend was also avoiding the attention of the smokers.

"Where's the damned ball?" Danny shrieked.

All eyes turned back to home-run country, from where Skippy was returning at a fairly quick clip for him. Not only was he returning without the one and only game ball, but he'd left his glove behind as well.

"For chrissake, Crenshaw," Greg muttered. Then, to the other eleven-year-olds, "Why'd you guys bring him along, anyway?"

"He's Danny's friend, not ours," Ben said quickly.

Danny wheeled to face Ben, but said nothing.

Ben glanced away, picked out the rapidly advancing Skippy.

"He looks funny," Trevor said.

He did, too. His eyes were wide and mouth slack rather than wrapped into some goofy grin. "So what do you guys want to do now?" Skippy asked as he came to a breathless halt at the outer edge of the infield.

Tony walked to within a few feet of Skippy, stared into his wide eyes like he was inspecting an interesting but none-too-appealing zoological specimen. He removed the cigarette stub from between his lips, dropped it, ground it to sparkly ash on the hard soil between the younger boy's feet. "Where's the ball?"

Skippy turned, paced, coughed into his hand. He made an issue of stretching his calves and rotating his hips, like he'd overextended himself on the jog in. "It's just that it's getting dark, you know. I don't think we ought to...I think we should go home." His voice climbing in pitch, he added, "I know what we can do. We can play Nintendo at my house. Greg and Tony can go first, since they're visiting."

Ben stared deep into the line of trees Skippy had departed so hurriedly. "You left your glove back there," he said quietly. Once the words were out, he felt as traitorous as he had when assigning the blame of Skippy to Danny.

"Just never mind, Crocker. All right?" Skippy's eyes blazed with a harshness that was rarely on display.

"Sorry," Ben mumbled.

Trevor ambled into the crooked circle that had gradually formed with Skippy its focal point. Trevor scrutinized the other boy like he was reading an interesting historical plaque. "No," he said softly, to no one in particular. "With the sun going down you might be too nervous to find the ball by yourself, but I can't think of a reason you'd leave your glove behind, too."

To the others, this statement had the effect of Columbo unmasking the least likely suspect as the perpetrator of the television season's vilest crime.

Ben thought, *He wouldn't leave his glove behind unless...*

Greg chuckled. "What is it, numbnuts? What did you see back there that scared you so much?"

The younger Luckinbill glared at the squirming outfielder. "Probably freaked out by a bat," he offered with undisguised disgust.

"Are there any deer around here?" Danny asked. "I bet he heard a deer crashing through the woods."

"Or a dog," Ben added.

Skippy was paying little attention to all of these opinions. His head kept turning toward center field. Ben could hear him muttering, though maybe only to himself, "You guys, I don't think we should—"

Trevor never let him finish. He said, "It's the dream, isn't it, Skippy."

The others waited. Skippy turned to face Trevor, twice peeking over his slumped shoulders toward the outfield. "No way," he finally said firmly. "There's no way I'm going back there."

Tony said, "What the hell are you squid-brains talking about? What dream?"

"Oh, yeah, Skippy's dream," Danny said breathlessly.

"The tunnel and whatnot," Ben said. "What are you telling us, Skippy? That you found a tunnel out there?"

Skippy looked from face to face, searching for help wherever he could find it. "Don't make me go back there," he said.

Ben didn't hear this last plea. He was running to catch up with the others, all heading toward center field at a dead run.

Chapter Seven

Albert Durwood was, by far, the best show playing in Cleary by seven thirty that evening. In fact, Thad Crocker would have paid admission and another eight dollars for a jumbo hot-buttered popcorn and two soft drinks to catch this act live; if only it were an act.

But it was reality looking back at him from that cage. Reality of the worst kind.

He knew that the four people with him that evening undoubtedly felt the same way. They all sat, horrified, enthralled, eyes glued to a gray metal folding chair hastily requisitioned from the town hall next door.

Mass murderer Albert Durwood was staring back out at them in living, breathing color. Just sitting there on his narrow bed, leaning against the cinder-block cell wall and studying the small crowd studying him. There was a dreamy, glazed look in his eyes. A smile pulled at his thick, red lips. Thad couldn't help wondering if he'd worn that same slack, wet smile while wiping out his entire family.

Thad watched one small, gray moth land on those wet lips and brush its tattered wings into the thick, soft moistness. It fluttered away only when the lips parted to speak.

In a very low voice, Albert Durwood said, "You've got to invite the yellow moon in. It needs door openers, so suck it right into your pitiful lives. It wants to be wanted." Durwood chopped off a sharp burst of laughter, either to ironically underscore his solemn pronouncement or to belittle his listeners for taking him so seriously.

Thad forced his eyes from the killer to watch the faces of the others. He saw his own emotions mirrored four times: horror mingled with uncomfortable fascination, the shameful thrill that prickles every newspaper reader who takes in the day's torture slayings with barely suppressed glee.

Face it, he thought. They all read the front-page Teenage White Slavery Serial Rape and Murder Ring story before tackling the Paris economic summit in the business section.

Hey, human nature stinks.

"What are you talking about, man?" Kerri barked, referring to Durwood's last—and only—pronouncement. If anyone could get anything out of the man, it was likely to be the scowling town manager.

"Don't expect it to make sense," Tom Luckinbill said, his voice no more than a murmur. "Tell 'em, Jeff."

The young cop cleared his throat. "The DA I talked to in Louisville had a lot to say concerning Mr. Durwood. Guess he's a local celebrity. Used to be a city housing inspector, married for like twenty years...kind of a walking attitude problem for quite some time, but nothing serious."

Durwood watched. Grinned as if in approval of the beginning of his biography. Thad flicked at a moth gently nuzzling his ear, then cringed at the possibility of it being the same one that had landed on the killer's lips.

"Last couple years, though," Jeff continued, "Durwood starts acting funny. All kinds of complaints about coworkers ganging up against him. He files a couple lawsuits against the city, calls the police a bunch of times on his neighbors: music too loud, kids too loud. One of his own kids runs away from home."

"Insisted a Fourth of July fireworks show was just a cover so his enemies could blow him away," added Kerri, who'd apparently already been briefed. "Damn these moths," she added.

Jeff spoke up a little louder, as if anxious to resume control of the attention-grabbing report. "Once he beat his wife bad enough to send her to the hospital. That was because he heard her whispering to the dog, training it to attack him."

"Wonderful," Thad said. The back of his neck tickled. He moved quickly and slapped away the chalky remains of a slow flying insect.

"Should have blown him away rather than bring him in," said the fifth spectator, a Cleary cop named Baylog.

Tom shook his head. "You did the right thing, Mark. Nice arrest."

The middle-aged cop frowned at the praise. "Wasn't hard. Way he was driving, I knew he was drunk or fucked—sorry, Kerri—messed up."

"Did he identify himself?" Thad asked.

Baylog shook his head. Slapped his knee, utterly destroying a moth in a puff of dust. "Tell you the truth, at that point I wasn't even sure he knew how to speak. I could tell right away he was one of our out-of-towners and had no business driving that mile-long Lincoln with Kentucky plates."

"We traced it, found out it belongs to a doctor at some Fruitcake Manor near Louisville," Tom explained. "He was the head guy at the place where Durwood wound up after he really went off the deep end. Anyway, Jeff and Kerri started making phone calls and ended up doing a whole lot of listening to this Louisville prosecutor. By the way, they're going to work overtime on the paperwork and Jeff's got a call out to a district judge. We got a bunch of people trying to find out who's responsible for taking him back: FBI, US Marshals, state of Ohio, state of Kentucky, whatever. We don't have experience with this sort of thing. Be nice if we had some legal assistance of our own right now, but with Justine Pope on vacation...we'll get this fuckball off our hands as soon as possible. That's all I can say."

"Sounds like more paperwork than this asshole's worth," Officer Baylog rumbled.

"Speaking of which," Tom said, "you'd better fill some out, then get out of here, Mark. I need you out on the streets tonight."

The big officer grunted. After he left with one final glare at the prisoner, Jeff Smith continued the story he'd no doubt warmed up to. "He quit his job one day, Durwood did, saying 'they' were taunting him from the bathtub drain at a place he was inspecting."

Thad's throat tightened. He was reminded of his own drain, the one in his basement. He watched two more gray moths land on the smiling prisoner. One rode his left eyelid while the other disappeared up a nostril.

Someone gasped.

Albert Durwood chuckled. "Yellow moon," he croaked. His voice sounded pinched, like a man talking with one stuffed nostril. He rocked back and forth on his narrow cot.

Tom Luckinbill called out, "Jeff, what's with all the goddamned moths?"

Now they all looked up, all seemed to become suddenly aware of the fluttering sounds, like tattered whispers, all around them. Thad could detect erratic flight only when observed out of the corner of an eye.

They all watched as three more landed on Albert Durwood's face.

"Then what happened?" Thad asked quietly. He focused his attention on a blank cinder-block wall in the left corner of the tiny cell.

The young cop faked a laugh, like he could lighten the impact of his next words. "One night he took out his wife and three young kids with a baseball bat."

Tom twitched in his chair. "Baseball?" He glanced quickly at his watch. "What time's it get dark these days?"

Jeff shrugged. "Nine, maybe. Why?"

The chief slowly stood. "Nothing. Just...baseball. It reminded me, I think Greg and Tony went to Waylock Park to hit a few."

Thad jumped up, digestive acid biting his stomach lining.

The police chief caught his eye. "Your kid's out too, huh?"

Thad tried to think. "Last I knew. Think Megan said they were going to meet up with your boys." The words left his mouth with difficulty, so intent was he on sounding calm.

The chief waved off a couple moths. "Jeff, send a car to Waylock Park. Have them pick up Greg and Tony and whoever they're with. I want every single one of those boys dropped off on his own doorstep, deposited straight into the hands of his folks. Tell the parents to expect them, and if no one's home, bring them here. Got it?"

Thad was already grabbing for the wall phone in the corridor, but having a hard time remembering his own number. His mind kept picturing Ben's game being crashed by a stranger with glazed eyes and his own ball bat. A friend of Albert Durwood's, just breaking in to take a few swings.

Something fluttered raggedly in his ear.

Chapter Eight

"I'm telling you guys," Skippy began for what seemed like the dozenth time. He was sitting in the long outfield grass, just before the line of trees that granted automatic home runs. His arms were crossed, skinny legs splayed oddly. He didn't finish his statement; didn't have to. He'd already cajoled, threatened, bribed, and warned the others away from the damned thing, but nothing had worked.

Ben couldn't figure out Skippy's attitude. Not only had it been the boy's discovery, but he'd predicted it in a dream, for chrissake. A prophecy foretold in front of witnesses, so he wasn't bullshitting anyone. If it were Ben all this had happened to, he'd for sure be displaying a bit of well-earned cockiness right now.

Greg's first words concerning the discovery didn't sound nearly as awestruck as Ben had felt. He merely said, "So what's the deal? What did you guys bring me out here for? This?"

Ben could tell that Greg wasn't feeling as casual as he'd like the others to think he was. His was the flippant kind of remark you make when you don't want someone to know they've come up with a find so good it can't possibly be topped, but you're too unsettled to come up with a better put-down.

Greg's words had the desired effect on Skippy, though. He jumped to his feet and stomped right up to the front of the thing. "What do you mean, 'what's the deal'?" he demanded, face flushing. "I suppose shit like this happens to you all the time."

Ben winced at Skippy's tone of voice. He sounded like he didn't know he was talking to Greg Luckinbill.

Greg chuckled. He was standing, one hip jutting out toward Skippy in a body language taunt. "Well, little man. Seems to me you brought us out here to stare at a storm drain."

As if Greg's mention of the thing reminded Skippy of where he was, he stepped back while keeping its yawning black mouth in sight. "I'm out of here," he said.

If you didn't know the park real well, you'd respect Greg Luckinbill's cold logic. It was just a storm drain or culvert or something, a horizontal hole stabbing through a section of ground where it rose into a short hill running parallel with the line of trees. It was made of concrete, or seemed that way at the time. When Ben moved an ear close to it, he could hear the occasional drip of water echoing far into the distance, a sound that struck him as natural and even comforting.

"Of course the problem is that it wasn't here before," Ben said, figuring that the point should be made just for the record.

"Who's walking back with me?" Skippy asked rather suddenly and emphatically.

Greg's lips tightened. Ben knew he was trying hard to argue Ben's last comment, but didn't know how. The kids in town all knew every inch of Waylock Park—even the Luckinbills, who only visited Cleary part of the time since moving to Columbus after The Divorce three or four years ago. "All right," he said after a long pause. "The city just put it in, then."

"Why?" It was Trevor, always good for a good question.

"Why not?" Greg's scowl dared anyone to answer him.

Trevor cleared his throat. "Well, it's just that I don't see any real reason for there to be one here. What's it for, anyway?"

Ben thought about it. The concrete tunnel before them was the sort of thing you saw all the time everywhere. You just accepted them, like nostril hairs and yellow traffic lights. What was it for?

"It's a storm drain," Danny said.

"No, a culvert," Ben replied.

"Whatever it is," Tony said, "it wasn't here before we began playing ball. And I didn't see anyone putting it in."

As they all thought about that together, Ben could feel the fear prickling its way up the back of his scalp.

"The most interesting thing," Trevor said quietly, "is that it was in Skippy's dream."

The boys backed away, even the Luckinbills.

"See you guys, I'm out of here," Skippy called out shrilly. He hadn't had to retreat with the others, as he was already maintaining a very respectful distance from the tunnel. "Now come on, who's going home with me? It's getting dark, you guys. I'm not joking anymore."

As if he ever had been.

Danny began to moan in the world's worst ghost impression while Tony hummed the theme music to *The Twilight Zone*.

"Stop it!" Skippy shouted.

Trevor stood up—he'd been squatting in front of the tunnel, squinting into it—and tramped up the hill toward the rear of the thing.

"Let's check it out," Danny said, following Trevor's lead.

Ben and the others fell in behind the first two, except for Skippy, who was still shouting his warnings and his goodbyes.

On account of the setting sun and the dense foliage, the boys didn't find much but shadows on the other side of the hill. Ben could barely make out Trevor, hands on hips, walking back and forth, leaning into a bush, kicking a branch aside, peering in, standing back.

"Help him," Greg ordered. "We got to find where the other end comes out."

What followed was the best time of the evening, the only good time that night. Danny fell into a prickly bush, swore, then threatened to go home when Ben and Tony laughed at him. To this, Tony added an earnest account of the one-armed chain-saw murderer who lived in the bushes, and Danny said he didn't believe a word of it, but that he was going home too. Neither of them did, though. Skippy refused to go anywhere unless someone else left with him. Ben figured that the other boy actually had a sort of love-hate relationship with his discovery. Danny, for his part, decided he could stick it out if Skippy could. So the six thrashed on in search of the back end of the mysterious tunnel.

Impossibly, they never found it. The vegetation grew dense back there, but it wasn't exactly a rain forest. Finally giving up the search, they stumbled back over the hill, sat down in front of the culvert or tunnel or storm drain and stared into the black circle.

"This is crazy," Tony finally sputtered. "We played here all day and that damned thing just wasn't here."

"Don't be retarded," his brother said. "Of course it was. We just didn't see it."

"Unh-uh. It wasn't here." This came from Skippy, and he seemed too bewildered to worry about contradicting Greg.

Ben said, "Maybe it's some kind of optical illusion or something."

"Would you please explain what that means?" Trevor asked with dripping sarcasm. Ben's best friend didn't handle confusion well. It tended to make him cranky.

Ben said, "Well, if you've got a better idea—"

"Shut up," Tony hissed. "Listen. What's that?"

After a second, Skippy said, "Hey, if you guys are trying to scare me—"

"Wouldn't be the hardest thing in the world," Danny said.

"It's music," Trevor said.

In another few seconds, the truth of Trevor's words became apparent to all. It *was* music, but it had to be some kind of acoustic effect like what Ben had learned about in school, when sound waves bounced around all crazylike, sounding like they were coming from where they weren't. That was the only way he could explain the tinkle of ice cream truck music coming out of the tunnel.

Not even Trevor had another explanation. He just stood there with his mouth as open as everyone else's and stared into the tinkling void.

For a very long time afterwards, Ben Crocker was to regret his next boisterous words, but at the time they seemed logical enough. "The

47

only way we're going to learn anything is by crawling through the mother."

Later he'd wonder why no one had suggested that earlier, hadn't even raced for the right to be the first one through. He'd think, *They knew...we all knew. We just didn't know we knew.*

But that was later.

Six pairs of eyes stared into the awaiting darkness.

"No possible way," Skippy said conversationally.

Ben had himself almost convinced that he could see shadowy light far, far back in the inky blackness of the tunnel's throat. He leaned in for a closer look, only to be attacked by the sound of his own nervous breathing, augmented many times over as it bounced off the unknown lengths of the thing's walls and hurtled back out at him like the harsh panting of a thousand frightened boys. Ben backed away.

Greg, none too enthusiastically, said, "We gotta go in."

Ben felt his scalp tingling again. He loved Greg's idea as much as he hated it. The tunnel-culvert-storm-drain had that kind of pull on him, and likely on the others as well.

They knelt before the opening. Ben squinted hard, sure that he'd see more than shadow-black if only he concentrated, which was the reason he let his eyes scrunch up so that they only let in sharp slits of light.

Trevor moved away and came back with a piece of shale the size of his fist. He curled his fingers around it. The others silently moved aside so that Trevor could squat as close to the mouth of the tunnel as anyone dared. He wound up and whipped the rock into the black opening.

Ben and the others heard it clanging off of a wall, the sound echoing back at them like a rock attack rather than a single missile.

When the reverberations ceased, the shale lay nearly out of sight. Ben could see where the edges had crumbled away against the hard tunnel surface.

Ben wondered what he and the others had been expecting: an explosion with a fiery show of sparks, a demonically driven red-hot missile hurtling back out at them at the speed of light, or perhaps for the thing to simply pop out of existence, rivaling any gimpy trick Penn and Teller could perform.

Whatever he and the others had subconsciously expected, they were to be disappointed.

"I don't care," Skippy said, as if rebutting a statement no one had made. "I'm still not going in there."

Then we'll poke out an eye

And leave you to die...

Ben shook his head like he could dislodge the words his mind was forming to go with the snatches of scratchy, canned music that the summer breeze sucked out of the tunnel.

Danny started to giggle quietly, and whispered, "Oh, shit."

Tony punched Ben in the shoulder. "Okay," he said, chuckling. "Your idea, you lead."

Ben tightened, tried to brace himself, force his body to take that first step.

Skippy said, "You guys still aren't listening to me. I said I'm—"

Greg said, "I'll go first." It sounded like something pleasureless, something he *had* to do, being the oldest and all.

Ben moved gratefully aside, breaking his view of blackness and spider webs.

"Come on," Greg said, duck-walking forward. "None of you wimpos had better cut out."

"I'm no wimpo," Danny mumbled.

Skippy just laughed, a high, desperate sound. He'd been called worse.

Trevor slithered into the tunnel a split second before Ben, and after Tony. *Great*, Ben thought. That left him ahead of only Danny and Skippy, and what did that make him but leader of the wimpo squad?

Your body will stiffen and bloat

Your soul will leave you and float

But nowhere near Heaven, oh, no

To Hell you're bound, to Hell you'll go

Ben stopped. "Ssh. You guys hear anything?"

Skippy wailed, "Ben, quit trying to scare me, or I'm going home. I don't even know why I'm here."

"Just ignore it," Tony said. His words sounded muffled and flat coming from the tunnel. "It's got to be a radio or something."

Ben let out the breath he didn't even know he was holding. "Just hurry up and go," he told the three in front. He closed his eyes as tight as his eyelid muscles would allow. If he had been able, he would have covered his ears as well, but he needed hands for crawling forward.

When he felt something lightly touching a knuckle, his eyes flew open and he gasped. Despite—or maybe on account of—his mood of abject terror, he giggled at his quick glimpse of the creature that had brushed against him.

It was going to take a hell of a lot more than some old gray moth to make him lose his cool around the Luckinbill brothers.

Chapter Nine

"Go ahead," Vern Withers said. "I can't wait to hear how you're going to handle this one."

Dinner at the in-laws no longer seemed so bad to Steve Addams, the twenty-seven-year-old newlywed. A shitload better than parking out in a homemade ball diamond in a cruiser with bigmouthed Vern Withers, who was sure to tell the entire Cleary police force what Steve thought he'd—what he had—seen out near that line of trees deep in the outfield.

"Come on," Vern said. "I dare you to call it in." The older man's grin was filled with mischief and bad teeth.

Steve picked up the police-band radio mike, licked his lips, and depressed the button. "Central, do you read? Car Four here, do you read?"

"Hey, what's up, Steve? You find the ten thirty-ones yet?" It was still Jeff dispatching, working an extended shift and asking about the missing persons. His voice sounded as fresh as it had earlier in the day, before the weirdos had started coming out.

Vern rested his elbows on the squad car hood by the passenger door, his veiny eyes dancing. The car ticked as it cooled.

Steve reached in and clicked off the spotlight switch. He felt ridiculous the way the light called attention to empty vegetation. He turned away from his partner, not really sure what that would accomplish. From this view, he could count three of the shadowy strangers limping aimlessly about the infield. One was probably a woman, carrying a loaded department store bag.

He got extended radio squelch for his hesitation. Then he heard, "Steve, you okay? What's up?"

"Yeah, Jeff," he answered quickly. "Just, uh, no...we haven't found the kids yet. We're at Waylock Park now and don't see anyone but, you know, more of *them*."

Steve Addams was tired. He wasn't even supposed to work till Tuesday, which was why he was wearing a Cincinnati Bengals jersey and running shorts. Both pairs of blues were at the dry cleaners, for chrissake.

"It's okay," Jeff was saying, as if he could feel Steve's mood. "Just keep looking. Tom and Kerri are a little concerned with all the crazies. Can you blame them?"

Steve ended the transmission, then stared down his partner. "All right, I didn't say anything."

Vern's eyes darted to the infield, then returned to Steve. "Didn't figure you would." He sounded almost disappointed.

"I saw what I saw," the younger cop said sullenly.

Vern turned and kicked at tall grass near a short incline. "Right. You saw a couple kids climb into a culvert." He pointed with a meaty fist. "Right here?"

Tennis shoes and skinny pink legs, more than one set of them, disappearing into a storm drain or something. Yeah, that's what he'd seen. Just a quick glimpse. He'd lowered his eyes for a second to grab the radio mike and report the ten thirty-one-A: missing persons found. But...

He stared down the high grass, stunted bushes and sparse weeds, daring nature to keep the tunnel from view. "I saw what I saw," he said again with exaggerated calm.

Vern wasn't listening. He was glaring at the wandering wastes rummaging uselessly about the infield. "Night of the Fucking Dead," he growled.

Chapter Ten

Yellow moonlight's what they found on the other side, or at least that came as close as anything else to describing what they saw out there.

Most of Ben's time while worming his way through the tunnel had been spent tracking threatening patterns from the void. The near-total absence of light filled his vision with inky movement and his mind with black doubts.

Grunting noises echoed off those hard walls as the others crawled uncomfortably forward. Sometimes Ben heard the ice cream music drawing them closer, and sometimes he didn't. The cool, hard surface felt wet on his palms, but when he held a hand against his cheek, the skin was dry.

"Been a damned long time, hasn't it?" Tony asked no one.

"Almost there," Greg answered, or at least Ben thought it was Greg. The voices ahead of him came back flat and tinny, like through walkie-talkies that never quite work beyond Christmas.

Then one of the Luckinbill brothers said, "Oh, Christ," real low, but not quite a whisper. Danny, from behind, started singing "Ooh hoo-oo, the bogeyman," but no one laughed.

Ben kept crawling, out of habit—like he'd been moving that way forever—until he bumped into Trevor, who'd bumped into Tony, who didn't even swear, so Ben knew something was wrong.

And that's when he saw yellow moonlight.

That might not have come close to the actual shade, but when you try comprehending something physical, you generally start with a color, and yellow was the only one that came halfway to mind.

What Ben saw—and he was only staring at a piece of the scene, a little patch between Tony's armpit and Trevor's shoulder as they all scrunched around the tunnel opening—was trees and bushes and night sky. Pretty much what he'd seen on the other side, only here it was all wrong. The trees were gnarly and spiky, without too many branches, while the bushes had too much foliage. Little things like that, things that shouldn't have mattered...

And big things. Like yellow moonlight, a color that never was meant to be. It washed over the scene, placing them all in a television world where the tint controls had run amuck.

"Let's go back," Ben said, for once not the least bit afraid of looking afraid.

No one answered. They just kept peering from that culvert, as if it kept them safe like the first-base bag in a pitchout.

"What is it? Let me see." Danny pushed his way forward, blowing bad breath Ben's way as he talked down his neck. "C'mon guys, get outta the way. Let me see."

"Let's listen to Ben," Skippy said.

What Greg growled next, Ben figured, was just to show everyone how unlike Skippy he was. "Who's chickenshit? Tony?"

"Hell no." His brother's answer came back fast and hard.

"Trevor?"

There was a long pause, then, "Unh-uh."

"Ben?"

He wanted to pass up that question. He wanted to be home in bed with a cool summer breeze floating through the open window, his folks talking and laughing real low in the living room, the way they talked when Ben and his sister Jessie were sleeping. "No way," he lied. "I'm not scared."

"Danny?"

"Forget it," Danny answered. "I don't even know what the hell's out there. You faggots are in my way."

And finally, from Greg, "Skippy? Are you chickenshit?"

Of course they all knew the answer to that one, even Skippy. "I'm not going back alone," he answered quickly, settling the issue on a technicality.

So they all stepped out together under a yellow moon.

No one made a sound as they squirmed onto solid ground. Part of the reason was that the ground wasn't so solid. It was spongy, but not muddy. Marshmallowey, Ben judged it. Although they'd sink nearly to their ankles with every slow step, their feet came up—almost bounced up—clean and dry.

"Gross," Ben said.

His voice seemed to crack the clean air, like it was the first thing that had been there for a while. A long while.

"We on the other side of Miller Road?" Danny asked.

Tony shook his head. "You'd be able to hear the highway."

It didn't surprise Ben until a second later that he'd been able to clearly see Tony shake his head. They'd crawled through near darkness, but here—wherever *here* was—the six of them nearly glowed despite the black condition of the sky.

The difference was that bright and unnatural moonlight.

The other thing that struck Ben was how right Tony was. They would have been able to hear traffic sounds if they'd come out on the far end of the park.

That was the point where they all seemed to decide at once that they'd seen enough: the moonlight, the springy soil, the virgin air and those spiky black trees. It might be a great place to explore in the morning after a long night's sleep. Lousy place with the lights off.

They all turned back to the tunnel.

It wasn't there.

Someone made a sound, a sharp cry, and Ben froze. It wasn't Skippy or Danny. It was Greg. That was bad news, about as bad as it could get.

They all just let that cry hang in the air while they stared stupidly at the hillside a step or two away, where the tunnel used to be.

That's when they heard the beast.

Chapter Eleven

Screw the ACLU.

Tom Luckinbill's words of several minutes before still hung heavy in the air as Thad awaited the roundup. He watched as each of the town's four working squad cars dumped fresh loads of not-so-fresh street types into the combination police station and local lockup.

Thad forced himself to watch as each male—and occasional female—was led in. The mayor was looking for bloodstains, and fervently hoping not to find any.

He and Kerri would each ask the same question: did you see a bunch of young boys playing baseball?

It got so that Tom was surprised at receiving a coherent reply. Usually, they ignored him; at other times they might have been responding to a question put to them months ago. Infrequently, he'd see a glint of humanity in a rheumy pair of eyes and get a mumbled, "Didn't see no one." Often the glint faded even before the response was completed.

A woman sang a nursery rhyme.

A man with one leg argued a poker hand with his unseen opponent.

A black youth of maybe seventeen earnestly described a conversation he'd just had with Jimi Hendrix.

Tom Luckinbill caught Thad's attention and motioned him over to one corner, where he'd been conversing in low tones with Jeff Smith. Kerri, meanwhile, kept barking out her insistent questions to the newly incarcerated.

"What is it?" Thad asked, snapping at the police chief as if warding off the worst.

Tom held up a hand. "It's not bad news, exactly. Just...no news."

"Meaning...?"

"I think we have everyone off the streets we've seen so far. Something like thirty-four of them. No one seems unduly suspicious." He paused to sort out the unintentional irony of his words. "Comparatively speaking, that is. In other words, there've been no confessions, no bodies and no obvious signs of violence. We're still trying to ID most of them, but we haven't run across anyone else like Durwood yet, and he was one of the first ones caught. I bet we had him before the boys came up missing."

Thad wearily ran a hand through his hair. "Are we going to get help on this?"

Tom eyeballed his assistant. "Jeff?"

The young man's all-business attitude allowed room for not a trace of his usual good cheer. "We're still looking, but nearly positive there hasn't been a mass escape anywhere. The few we've been able to put names to and find records of have been on their own for some time. It's not a crime to be nuts. Durwood's the only one of his kind so far, and he didn't break out with anyone else."

"Back to my original question," Thad said firmly. "We going to get any help?"

"Uh, yes sir. Eventually. Kerri got on the phone to the FBI office in Cleveland or somewhere. They didn't seem real helpful concerning the influx of suspicious persons, but started listening when they heard about missing children. It's still early as far as they're concerned. If the kids are gone overnight, they'll send someone down first thing in the morning."

"Shit." Thad's head pounded.

Tom touched his shoulder, then quickly withdrew. It was the closest thing to a comforting gesture the police chief could extend. "I know how you feel," he said. "Remember, my boys are out with yours."

"Wish we knew that for sure."

Tom nodded. "Yeah." He crossed his arms. "Hate to have to suggest this, but do you think it's time to tell Megan?"

Thad crumpled up against a cork wall filled with posted schedules, calendars, flyers and memos. The station smelled ripe with humanity. He could hear giggles, mumbles and an occasional cry from thirty-four wretched shells.

He'd sounded casual enough the last time he called his wife to find out whether Ben had returned home. She hadn't grilled him then, but she'd still sounded suspicious and worried. This conversation would be different. Much worse in that the worst-case scenario might have already been played out.

Seeing that every desk telephone was occupied by a nervously chattering city employee, Thad exhaled impatiently, poked at a pocketed quarter and snatched a public phone from its wall mount.

Chapter Twelve

The sound fell in somewhere between a roar and a loud chuckle, without being either. As impossible to describe as yellow moonlight. Ben's leg muscles clenched so tight he could barely move.

Skippy said, "I'm going back," and that was almost funny.

"Sure thing," Danny whispered, his voice shaking like his body. "Whatcha gonna do? Catch a cab?"

"No. I'm going to call my dad."

That was hilarious, but it wasn't. It made Ben want to do exactly the same thing. He wouldn't admit it to the others, but he was wondering if maybe there wasn't a pay phone somewhere.

"Oh, sure," Danny said, like he was reading Ben's thoughts, only he was talking to Skippy. "You got a quarter? See a phone? Why don't you bring us back a pizza?"

Skippy turned to that empty green hillside where a tunnel used to be, and started to thrash around looking for it while the others huddled close together.

"There's nothing there," Danny said.

"Gotta be," Skippy replied, still looking, pacing, head bent.

Greg said, "He's right. It has to be there. Doesn't make sense for it to disappear like that. Just doesn't make sense." Greg glared in the direction of the beastly scream, as if belligerence could overcome facts.

Skippy scrabbled away at the hillside like a dog uprooting a lawn.

"Maybe this is a secret government place," Trevor said. "Like where they store nuclear missiles and no one in town's ever seen it but us."

"Maybe," Ben said, more for something to say than out of a sense of belief. He doubted even the government could make culverts disappear. The idea, from the brainiac of the pack, seemed wackier than his own optical illusion theory of what seemed like a long time ago, but he was in no mood to argue.

"Or maybe we're just imagining all this," Tony said. "Say they put something in our water or something, and they're testing us to see what we do."

Ben liked that theory even less than Trevor's. Who were "they"? And why would "they" do this to a bunch of kids?

Skippy seemed to appreciate it, though. He stopped digging. His face brightened under the strange moonlight. Ben could clearly see every premature worry line. "Yeah, that's it, isn't it, Tony? You're wrong, Ben. I don't think Tony's idea is a bad one at all."

Ben frowned. "I never said it was."

"Well, you were thinking it."

Now it was Trevor's turn to frown. "Skippy, how'd you know what Ben was thinking?"

Skippy paused, frozen in the process of scaling that short hill. "Don't know. Just that...things are different over here. I'm different." He paused to think about what he'd just said, then looked really scared. "It's not the kind of different I like."

"The dream," Trevor said quietly. "The one you had last night."

"This whole thing just isn't happening," Skippy said, drowning out Trevor's words. "That's it. And if I go over the hill again—"

"Don't." It was Greg, but he didn't sound right. It was a plea, not an order he was issuing.

Skippy ignored it. "Come on, you guys," he said, with something like thin hope in his thin voice. "Let's go home."

Ben didn't say anything; no one did.

Skippy looked at the others, and his eyes got hard like Ben had never seen them before. He seemed to know he was about to go it alone. Then he scrambled over the hill, waving one arm forward like Vic Morrow in those old *Combat* reruns.

"Don't go," Greg said again, but by then it was too late. Skippy was gone, and no one followed. Maybe no one believed he'd really take off like that. They stood there waiting for something to happen, and of course something did. The crisp air was pinched by a high-pitched wailing sound. It might have been Skippy, but Ben didn't think so. He didn't think Skippy had gotten the chance.

Then silence. The quiet was the worst part. Too much thinking time.

Once when Ben was small, he'd gotten up in the middle of the night to go to the bathroom. He'd spent most of that evening scaring his highly scareable sister Jessie, so that night as he climbed back into bed and was about to tuck in his pivot foot, something reached out from underneath and grabbed it.

Ben's elevated sense of terror had actually becalmed him. His whole body just sort of let loose, and for one impossible second he floated away from the terror, light as air and just as untouchable.

Of course, it had been a vengeance-minded sister under the bed that night, and for the three years since then, Ben honestly believed he'd been through the worst.

Until he heard the thing that got Skippy. At that point he wished he could make a deal with God and have Jessie reach out and grab his ankle every night if he could erase what was happening to Skippy.

He didn't know how many millions before him had made similar promises, begged as irrationally for similarly impossible reprieves from the unalterable, the inevitable.

Maybe the boys—five of them now—would have stayed there forever, crouched under the hillside, sometimes staring at where the tunnel used to be and trying to avoid seeing the nasty-looking trees and shrubbery, trying real hard not to hear anything, if Tony hadn't kicked in.

He stuck his hand into a mass of shrubbery and pulled out a mean-looking walking stick, thick as a ball bat, and swung it like it was some cave-man weapon. All the while he frowned the way only a Luckinbill could frown.

"Come on," he said, and they all knew what he had in mind. They went because they had to get Skippy back, or at least try. More than that, they stayed together because it was less dangerous than wandering away from the pack.

Skippy had proven that.

Chapter Thirteen

She saw a killer lurking behind every glazed eye, a strangler in every gnarled, dirt-stained hand; even those of the few, toothless hags of women. If she could have beaten the information from the assembled insane, she would have. Her adrenaline rush demanded such activity, but somehow she held back.

She concentrated first on the multitude packed into the crowded cells on the east side of the building, ignoring—or sincerely trying to ignore—the one whose criminal reputation had earned him the comfortable solitude of the entire west-end cell bank. He could see her, though. Was he watching her right now, smirking with deadly secrets?

The woman with Megan perhaps read some of her horrible thoughts, for Kerri Upshaw now braced Megan's trembling body with a strong arm.

"They probably know nothing," Kerri said. "Tom and the others haven't found a single reason to believe anyone here's involved. It's most likely just a coincidence."

Coincidence. What a lovely thought: that thirty-some ragged strangers happen to call Cleary home on the exact day that Ben and five of his friends disappear. She stared into the crowded cells, looking for the first sign of intelligent life.

"What is it?" she quietly asked no one. "What's going on out there?"

"I know," a voice replied. And again.

The words, repeated a half dozen, now a dozen times, came from a very short, very stout woman wrapped in what looked like a beaver fur.

Once, perhaps, it had been worth something. Now it displayed layers of alley dirt.

"Jesus," Megan said, despondency turning the word into a whisper.

"Nope," the tattered woman answered. "Melba McCann."

At another time, Megan would have laughed. She would have felt a sense of tenderness for the stranger, but she'd packed her warmer emotions away, hidden them in strong wooden crates in the dungeon of her mind, where they'd stay until her son returned.

Megan and Kerri had volunteered to watch over the prisoners for the police, whose time was spoken for in a record number of ways. So they stood. Paced. Leaned. Whispered. Watched.

There were five incarcerated females so far, and not enough cell space to segregate them from the men. Each of the two east-end cells, not much larger than an average bedroom, held sixteen or seventeen people.

Most of the detainees huddled on the floor, muttering, seemingly oblivious to the others milling about. The accumulation of unwashed flesh within seamy clothing was producing a raw and disconcerting amalgamation of smells, including a faint but insistent hint of human waste.

Of course, conditions didn't have to be quite so crowded. There was an entire empty cell on the other side of the narrow hallway. The cell next to Albert Durwood with the flushed face, high forehead and thick, red lips.

Megan turned her head nervously. He was watching her or perhaps seeing nothing at all. He sat straight up on his bunk, his short, thick legs barely reaching the floor. His chest and shoulders were broad, his hair greasy, the color of old pennies.

Tom Luckinbill hadn't discussed his reasons for locking no one in the cell next to the famous one, but Megan instinctively understood. In an emergency you could arrest and detain the suspicious, could even justify shoe-horning them into cubicle cells, but it would take a major absence of human compassion to move them next to an animal like Albert Durwood.

She returned her attention to the others, even edged closer to the bars, ignoring the sharp, raw smells of the street-diseased and chronically unwashed, and forced herself to hear their mutterings. Maybe someone knew something.

A man with gray, matted hair and a festering bald spot was braying the Lord's Prayer. When he got to the end, he picked up the prayer's beginning line without missing a beat, so that the enthusiastic chant became as timeless as the god he commemorated.

"Swear t'God," said one, a short man who could have been thirty or fifty. "I was there, I seen Willie Mays catch it like it weren't nothing. Came flying in from center, ball's almost outta the park, by God, but he reeled it in..."

A woman in a babushka scarf and eyeglasses with one empty lens spoke very calmly to ethnic ghosts in an Eastern European language.

A black man with one arm said something that was as indistinguishable as the woman's comments except that it seemed to include frequent references to Santa Claus.

Megan moved slowly from the cell to stand next to Kerri, who was facing the adjoining one.

"I've heard these people before," Megan said quietly. "Not around here, but in big cities. Heard, but never listened."

"All of us, same way," Kerri admitted with a sad smile.

"Do you think any of it makes sense to them? I mean, the guy who's talking about Willie Mays and a baseball game probably thirty years in the past, does it hold some kind of rational meaning for him, or do you think...what is it?"

Megan's interruption of her own words was due to the quizzical frown she was receiving from the older woman.

Kerri asked, "Who mentioned anything about Willie Mays and baseball?"

Megan jerked a thumb toward the cell she'd just walked away from.

Kerri lifted an eyebrow. "The old guy?"

"Old. Young. Who can tell anymore. But he's the one. Why?"

Kerri turned back to the cell nearest the two of them and pointed a finger at a man in his early twenties with long black hair. The man, like most of the others, was mumbling. Megan strained to pick the words out of the overall jumble.

"You didn't see no Willie Mays in no ballpark in Dakota, you liar. The whoppers you tell..."

Megan backtracked the six or eight steps to the adjoining cell.

The short man of indeterminate age was wearing a green stocking cap. He sat on the edge of the bunk with four or five others, facing away from the long-haired kid in the next cell. His voice was low, the sounds emanating for no one's apparent benefit but his own. "You a liar and a bastard, calling me a liar. I knowed Willie Mays since we was kids. Hanged out together, man. I won't tell you no more 'cuz you got no respect for the truth."

Megan again moved back toward Kerri.

The long-haired kid: "Yeah, well, you hang out with niggers, makes you a nigger. But Willie Mays one nigger you don't know."

"They're in contact," Megan whispered.

"Ho, ho, ho."

It came from a man with a purple scar on his cheek.

At once Megan knew he was answering the black man who'd been talking about Santa Claus.

Kerri moved back and forth as Megan had. The older woman's face paled when their eyes locked.

"They can't possibly hear each other," Megan said, her own words nearly lost in the din. She clenched her arms to her body, holding herself together against a rising wave of panic.

Someone laughed behind her.

"But we're crazy, don't you know?" Albert Durwood said. "That's not explanation enough?"

Both women jumped at the sound of the man's voice. It was as thick as his lips, as watery as his eyes.

Megan forced herself to the man's cell. He was smiling. A yellow moth preened on his cheekbone. She stepped back as a fog of the flying creatures settled on the cell bars to inspect her. "What the—"

"We don't know," Kerri said. "It's got to be that there's a nest of them against that wall. But...don't get too close."

Megan ignored her. She gripped Durwood's bars and pressed her head against cold steel. Her fingers were tickled by the crisp touch of fluttery wings. "Where's my son? What's happening here?"

His blue—nearly colorless—eyes never left hers as he rubbed a fisted hand across his lips. Scraped off a twitching movement and examined it. Rubbed his fingers clean on a sleeve, leaned back, folded one leg comfortably over the other. "It's the yellow moon," he replied. "The gods of the drains are almost here. That's what's happening. Need I say more?"

He started to smile, then abruptly cancelled it. His rubbery mouth went hard, seemed to tremble. "The gods of the drains told me what to do, and everything that's followed, all that will follow, is what happens when you just open your heart, open your soul. I'm the one they called to lead them in, these others are just like"—he paused, surveyed his surroundings as if for the first time and smiled—"like moths before a flame."

"Talk to me," Megan snapped. "What do you know, what do they know?"

"Have you ever seen them? In their drains. Beauty and horror. Same thing. Beauty and horror."

She was losing him. His lips were still moving, but nothing more came out. His gaze had left her, had refocused somewhere in space.

Kerri stood behind her. "Megan, I think you should move away from there."

"They know something," she said. She twirled, faced the other shambling wrecks. "Something happened. Or...not yet, but it will. My God, we only call them crazy because we don't understand what they know. They don't either. They can't handle it, so this happens. They just break."

"There, there," a soothing voice answered. The woman shuffling to the front of her cell was the one in the ratty fur coat who'd called herself Melba McCann. "It's not so bad," the woman said, smiling pleasantly. Her hand snaked past the cell bars. It was caked with grime, five thick fingers ending in black stubs of nails. "You get used to it, dearie."

Megan let one of the old woman's broken fingertips touch her own, ever so slightly, and—

Once upon a time there was a little girl who never got enough attention from her mother and too much from her father The little girl tried to explain things to her mother, tried to form words describing the way she felt when late at night her bedroom door would creak open and the large shadow spilled over all of the other shadows and she could smell his strong, late-night tavern smell and he'd clear his throat and sit down heavily on her squeaky mattress and oh-so-quietly whisper her name and sweetly stroke one drawn leg and it would begin. Again. But when she explained, the words came out trembly and wrong and her fearful mother had little time for listening anyway.

So the little girl grew up and got married and had a little girl of her own and always watched her husband very, very closely, waking up every time he got up in the middle of the night, and only allowing herself the blind comfort of sleep when he came back to bed, her bed, their bed right after the toilet flushed.

He was a good enough man, this husband of Melba McCann and father of Tina. Spent a lot of time away, but usually had a job of one kind or another and never beat on mother or daughter, but Melba knew she'd catch him one day in the wrong bedroom and wondered how she'd handle it when it happened, and that took up an awful lot of her time.

She never told her husband about this fear of course, but it must have showed because she was always angry and his own anger simmered in that low-boil way of his. They fought with gaping silences until Tina moved away to remove the unspoken source of their angers

69

but by this time the anger was a hard, unbreakable shell so what did finally break was their marriage. Whatever it was that had finally sparked the last skirmish barely mattered.

With him gone, Melba could concentrate on her daughter, on Tina's wild ways with men, the girl supporting one harsh boyfriend after another with garter-belt tips at juice bars in the seediest sections of the seediest cities. So now Melba could spend her time with painful conjectures of what went wrong to make her daughter this way. She blamed the girl's father for finding his way into the wrong bed despite her motherly diligence, but mostly Melba blamed herself for letting the sordid illness of her own childhood infect the next generation as well.

These thoughts dug deep scars that only liquor could soothe. Not heal, but soothe.

The booze showed her the futility of her painful existence, and opened up a thousand avenues of mortal escape, but her own cowardice locked her in the land of the living with her self-loathing.

Which was when she began to hear the voices in the kitchen drain. They saved her dismal life, those voices. They understood. They promised relief, and Melba believed.

She told her daughter the stripper about those wonderful voices, but Tina, her own flesh and blood, refused to hear. Tina joined the other side, joined those plotting against her mother and all of the others like her by informing on her to a member of that group Melba came later to know as the most dreaded enemy of the true believers.

Tina's doctor nodded as if he understood every word Melba spoke, only she knew different because the gods of the drains had given her a most wondrous gift: the ability to read minds. It wasn't a perfect gift; it faded in and out like an old television set with aluminum-foil-wrapped rabbit ears. At times she picked up the unspoken with crisp clarity, but those times were rare and followed by longer periods of mental confusion that felt like driving through a tunnel with the radio shouting a blizzard of white noise.

This doctor, he wanted to put her in a hospital. He conferred with other doctors whose thoughts she sifted during her clever moments. She learned enough to know that it was time to follow the wise guidance of the gods of the drains and disappear until the new order could be established.

So Melba McCann drifted into the night, the most terrible time for her, since she knew what skulked about under cover of darkness: hulking night shadows smelling of liquor and foul desire. But she went because she had to find the source of those commanding voices.

On the streets, in the alleys, in abandoned buildings smelling of urine and cum, she found others like herself. Others who needed to talk only when the special powers faded or when too much liquor or too many drugs dulled their talent. They swapped incomprehensible theories, exchanged survival tips and drain-god mythologies before wandering away in an eternal search for others and yet others who could explain things better.

And then came a new message from the gods of the drains. The time is near, 'twas said. A great man has been found to lead the way, to bridge the gap between worlds. So they followed the voices like ragged shepherds under a guiding star.

To their destination, the place promised by the voices, they came together but alone in ones and twos and soiled coincidental clumps. They stumbled painfully toward Heaven, Paradise, Nirvana, Shangri-La.

Cleary, Ohio. As promised.

Only...different. Not as she'd imagined, but it was too late...too late...

She heard her name being called, beckoning her from the drains and tunnels and whispering, slithering shadows creeping out of a colorless fog. No, not colorless, but so colorful that there was no name to describe the shade her mind was seeing.

"Megan, dammit, snap out of it!"

She blinked, and then it was over and Kerri was pulling her away from the clutches of the woman named Melba McCann. The husky town manager's face was pasty and as sweaty as Megan figured her own must be.

"What is it?" Kerri demanded in a voice brittle with alarm.

The woman named Melba McCann seemed to shrug deeper into the folds of her ragged fur as she stepped to the back of her cell to squat in a corner. "Didn't used to be able to do that," she muttered. "See what happens when the yellow moon rises?"

They watched, each of the inhabitants of the cells, their eyes eager and briefly alive before flickering out as before.

"They know so much, these people," Megan said, wheezing as if she'd finished a marathon. She felt that all she knew or thought she knew was slipping away even as her mind chased down the scrambled bits of her new wisdom. "Some of what they know scrapes off on the so-called normal ones, the way thousands of tiny magnets working together might pick up a car."

Kerri Upshaw glared at her in frustrated ignorance, and Megan knew it was no use explaining. All she said was, "It's here, Kerri. I don't know what it is, but...it's here or on its way."

And it's got my son, Megan added to herself, the realization a piercing shriek in the privacy of her own mind.

Something small and gray and feathery tickled her lower lip.

Chapter Fourteen

Oh my oh my how her old heart fluttered. It was a shame that poor young woman out there was getting in such a dither over yellow moon, an occurrence that she herself had tried to understand for months, years.

Melba McCann shrugged and addressed the air around her. "We could maybe help the situation, you know, if these so-called normal folks would just let us."

She heard what sounded to her mind like the equivalent of harsh, bitter laughter. *"Sure, and admit that we're the sane ones? Not likely, that."*

"I know how hard it is," Melba thought. *"My own daughter... I tried until nearly turning as crazy as they all said I was to convince my very own flesh and blood that what I heard, I heard. What I saw, I saw. How far'd I get? Don't even ask."*

The old woman's mind heard what her ears couldn't: *"You ever see normal people talk the way we talk? Without even moving our lips if we don't wanna."*

And from somewhere else in the void: *"We all should be on with Jay Leno making millions of dollars, not locked away like animals just 'cuz we're different. 'Cuz we're smarter. 'Cuz we heard the news first."*

Melba McCann nodded, chortled happily as she slapped her shoulders rhythmically against the cell wall. She spoke, forgetting, as she and the others frequently did, the superfluousness of the spoken word, speech being such a hard habit to break.

"Now you're talking, brother. Or sister. No longer matters which, I guess. Tried telling my Tina how things were changing. Tried describing what I saw, what I heard, but it got all garbled up on account of my brain not knowing all the right words, so she just looked at me, my very own daughter. Just looked all sad and scared, and that's when she started mentioning me moving in with her and the kids. All nonchalant, like if she talks casual-like I'm not going to notice she thinks I'm nuts."

The old woman in the beaver coat giggled to herself and anyone else tuned in to her mindwave, perhaps the world's largest party line. "Now here's a woman, my Tina, who's been married and divorced twice. She got two boys with the first, a girl with the second and another girl with, who knows, maybe it's the Immaculate Conception, or so she'd like me to think. She's a thirty-six-year-old topless waitress with a coke habit and she going to take care of me, she says. And the world says I'm the crazy one."

Melba McCann gave that some private thought. She'd left Portland after Tina made her go see that young doctor who'd talked too slow and too quiet, the way you soothe a toddler out of a crying jag. If there was one thing worse than being baby-sat by a topless dancer, it was permanently moving into sterile white rooms and wearing nightgowns that don't fasten in the back.

All because you know what's out there.

Melba wrinkled her brow. Her mind could see the tunnel at the bottom of her bathroom drain, and the shadowy things that called to her in the middle of the night. How come so few others could see what was happening?

Melba...Melba, they'd call. *It'll be so good, like Heaven, only better.*

Then how come—? No, don't think about it.

She had to. She huddled into herself, trying to bend her scrawny butt muscles to fit the hard contours of the chipped tile cell floor. How come, she asked herself, she sometimes didn't feel so wonderful when she thought of how the world was going to change once that yellow moon worked its way overhead? And didn't feel at all good when she sneaked a peek into that other cell and saw the man who sometimes crept into those dreams of hers.

"*We're all like that sometimes,*" replied a silent voice she picked out of the void. "*All scared. We just try not to think about it. Okay, maybe things could be just as bad as they are now when the gods of the drains come out, but they can't be worse. So just quit thinking about it. You could go nuts.*"

Chapter Fifteen

By now it came as no surprise to Ben that they didn't find Waylock Park beyond the hill, but he was amazed at just how far from Cleary they'd wandered. As he peered into those dark woods on either side, he kept thinking about how brave Skippy had been. There was no way he would have taken that walk alone.

Ben could see all too clearly by the ghastly moonlight. The breeze, cooler and cleaner than on the other end of the tunnel, was setting all those spiny tree branches to work, prodding the five boys onto the one narrow path that wound deeper into the woods.

The leaves on the razor-sharp branches were hideously exotic; flat, and as broad as his head. The woods were thick with those trees, an umbrella of foliage that sucked up light like a black hole, but somehow Ben could still see much too clearly.

"Come on. We gotta find Skippy." Tony didn't sound anywhere near as decisive as his words.

They stepped onto the spongy path in two groups: first Tony, then everyone else, all jammed together so no one had to bring up the rear.

With no sense of direction and no destination, they walked. The path lapped at their heels like mud without moisture. Every bend held lurking calamity.

"This is interesting," Trevor said. His voice, too loud for the quiet woods, brought Ben and the others to a panicky standstill.

"What's interesting?" Tony snapped. "And it better be."

Trevor pulled something away from his shoulder and flicked it to the ground. "This sap here, or whatever it is." He nodded toward the thick blob he'd flung to the path in front of him.

Ben felt something fall heavily onto his neck.

Danny said, "Gross, Ben. What is it?"

Ben plucked it from his skin. It didn't want to leave. It was green and thick, like the blob Trevor had found. He flung it to the ground and watched the others do the same, all pulling and flinging green mucous from hair and skin.

Maybe Tony didn't see the thing that plopped onto his ear, or he had so many others to get rid of that he lost track of that particular blob; in any case, it wasn't removed in time, and Ben happened to be staring at it when it turned.

It didn't happen all at once, but gradually, patiently, as if turning from a green blob of snot into a hairy worm was the most natural progression in the world. By the time it squirmed toward Tony's jaw, it was nearly identifiable as a member—a very primitive member—of the animal kingdom.

"Ugh," Trevor said.

Ben opened his mouth. "Tony. You...you..." Nothing else would come out.

Tony felt the stares or he felt the worm. He blanched as he tore at the thing on his face.

It didn't just fall off as any other worm would. It held on with bunches of newly created, tiny appendages that looked too complicated, too strong to be insect feet.

"Ugh," Trevor said again, pretty much summing up Ben's thoughts of the moment.

Ben heard a *scritch* sound as the thing was finally pried from Tony's face. The older boy threw it down and beat it back to slime with his walking stick. He pawed the red, scratched part of his face as if it were a section he'd prefer doing without.

"Ohmigod." Trevor was the one who always managed to stay clean, no matter what the activity. If he feared anything, it was dirt. And green slime that turned to worms with hairy feet and stuck to the middle of his nose so that he had to look at it cross-eyed. "Ohmigod."

Trevor began ripping at his face, and in a matter of seconds Ben was doing the same, and so was everyone else. Live snot fell from the dead trees like green rain. Soon, thick, green crawlers, newborns, nestled in scalps and discovered mouths and ears and other warm places to grab onto and enter and call home.

Ben started to run, as did the others, though he was too distracted to care. He was batting and swearing and slapping and spitting and swearing some more, all the while trying to dodge the things as they fell. About as unlikely as staying dry in a downpour.

At first he just covered his head, closed his eyes, and blundered deeper into the woods. He'd grab at a wet crawler as soon as he felt it land, squish it between his knuckles and rip it away—sometimes taking skin as well, but it didn't matter. Nothing mattered but getting rid of the bastards.

One landed on his ear and began crawling in, its thousands of tiny legs nuzzling him. Ben could hear it breathing, panting like an overweight dog after a short run.

Ben dug it out, slammed it to the ground and burrowed his head into his arms. He closed his eyes and crashed from one ghastly tree to another, the path picking his destination.

He vaguely heard footsteps behind and in front of him, muffled shouts from his friends. Together—sort of—they wound deeper and deeper, twisting with the path. Ben finally gave up all hope of dodging the slime. He could only pick the hideous green things from his face and shirt and hair, rip them away in squirming clots, throw them and stomp them by the fistsful.

His chest was knotted. His feet refused to take another step along that clean-mud path that clutched, sucked at his shoes, trying to pull him down and make creature-stew of him.

And as suddenly as the slime rain began, it ended. They were out of the woods and in the biggest open field Ben had ever seen.

He fell to the rich green grass and lay moaning at the recent memory and the sting of his prickled cuts as he sucked down fresh, slime-free air. Someone else plopped beside him, and he could barely make out additional huddled figures a few yards farther upfield. They all lay gasping, picking at dying crawlers, and sobbing.

He knew there was something wrong about that field right from the first. He just couldn't accept yet another impossibility, but even with his eyes closed and mind elsewhere he saw and felt yellow moonlight that was yellower—if that was even the color at all—than at any time before. That was why Ben kept his eyes closed as long as he did. Even living snot provided a safer mental picture than yellow moonlight.

Danny retched next to him, green and thick, and that's what brought Ben back. Vomit was a mundane horror he could deal with. It was while he rolled out of the way that he looked up and saw.

Later, Ben felt that if there was one sight that whole evening he could have done without, it would be that of the moon. Even if he had to deal with the crawling slime creatures or the winged toad and the rest to come, he would do so without complaint if he could have just escaped sight of that awful yellow moon.

He'd seen full moons before, some so big that they'd been frightening in a totally inexplicable way. Some that had made his chest tight, they were so big.

But nothing like the one over that open field. Not that color, kind of a dead yellow-but-not-yellow tone that resembled nothing he'd ever even imagined. It seemed to infect their clothing, their hair, probably even their souls in a wash of color that could never be scrubbed out.

"Look at the mountains," Trevor whispered.

There are probably mountains and valleys and all that stuff on the normal moon, Ben thought. He could almost remember that from Mrs. DeVane's science class. But you're not supposed to see those things, not without a pretty powerful telescope. And you're damned well not supposed to see shadows where the mountains meet the valleys. If you can, there's something seriously wrong, folks.

He didn't notice the rest of that black sky right away, maybe would have missed it altogether except Trevor said, "The stars," his voice full and shaky.

It took Ben a moment to realize that his friend was talking about the stars that weren't up there. Just endless, cloud-free blackness. That big, horrible moon had swallowed everything else.

Ben didn't know how much he missed stars until they were gone with nothing to replace them but an absence so deep, so complete, so real that he had to quit looking before he fell in.

He cried some more, then. They all did, lost on that vast, moonlit field with the realization of just how far from home they really were.

Ben wasn't sure, but the yellow moon seemed to shift while no one watched, because all at once they looked up with the same fearful gaze. He couldn't have explained it, but the light moved. It had all been collected in that huge ball, but now it spread like a sort of light shadow, the negative of a shadow, away from the moon and across the black sky. Not with movement they could see, exactly, but Ben could feel it, or maybe just glimpse it out of the corners of terror-widened eyes.

It crawled down from the sky and swept toward the top of the field, moving like a spotlight whose form they couldn't quite make out. Then it stopped, and all the yellow moonlight focused very tight upon the crest where the field rose slightly. That one patch of ground became center stage.

It was where the toad monster was eating Skippy.

Chapter Sixteen

"Durwood's crazy," Tom Luckinbill said. "If you didn't already know it, all you'd have to do is watch him."

They were doing just that, Thad and Megan and Tom.

Watching for what? Thad wondered, not for the first time. He glanced at his watch, his stomach feeling like setting concrete. Time was an endangered commodity. It was dark out there and his boy was lost. If, as Megan suspected, this insane murderer knew anything at all about Ben's whereabouts…

"I'm trying to tell you," the police chief was saying, "we're getting nowhere with this numbfuck. We haven't got a reason to suspect Albert Durwood of anything beyond advanced insanity, and that's just not enough."

"Then you can ignore the fact that a serial killer shows up in Cleary the same time Ben disappears?" Megan snapped.

"Ben and five other boys, including my two," the police chief replied.

"Sorry," Megan said, but Tom brushed it off with a brusque shake of the head.

Thad added, "We're all sorry. It's been a long, weird day."

"Just for the record," Tom said, "Durwood's not a serial killer. His spree took place on a single evening, not over the course of weeks or months or years. That makes him a mass murderer. The difference as far as we're concerned is that he snapped once, so he doesn't have a history of killing people any time he gets a chance."

"Lovely distinction," Thad mumbled.

"What's he looking at?" Megan was nodding toward the thickly built prisoner who was bent and peering intently into the wall sink in his cell. He was muttering, maybe directing his conversation toward two slim moths circling overhead.

"Whatever it is, he's been doing it off and on for at least the last hour," Tom replied in a low rumble. "From the occasional tidbits of conversation we pick up, he's addressing the 'gods of the drains', something like that."

Thad's stomach twitched as his mind called up again the gauzy memory of his basement experience.

The police chief returned his attention to the married couple. "Listen, if I thought I could get answers by twisting his nuts with pliers, hand me my tool box. I'd have a pretty good time doing it too, because I'm just as upset about the kids as you are. But Durwood's not even in this world right now. God knows where he is.

"Anyway, it doesn't make sense he could wipe out six healthy boys without a weapon. Without a trace of blood. Without a single sign of violence to his clothing, his car or on his person. No scratches, bruises, broken nails, nothing to indicate he's recently had to put up a struggle. And no reported gunshots anywhere in town. It just doesn't add up. Sorry." Tom shrugged to mark the end of his long speech. Long by his standards, certainly.

Thad could feel his bunched muscles loosen ever so slightly as his wife wrapped an arm around him.

"I'm sure you're right," she told the police chief. "Mostly I want to believe you, I guess, but it does make sense. The bottom line, though, is that I don't have the faintest idea where Ben is. And with every minute that goes by..."

She didn't finish. Didn't have to. Tom nodded his agreement.

That's when Albert Durwood cleared his throat, looked up to fully acknowledge their presence for the first time. His wet eyes brightened and a red-lipped smile parted the lower quarter of his face.

Thad didn't think he was going to like whatever the killer had to say, and he was right.

"The gods of the drains, they're eating your children's tender young flesh today. I hope they save some for me."

Chapter Seventeen

Ben Crocker was experiencing a first: fright so intense that it actually erased the sensation of fear. He just watched, the smallest details sticking in his mind like pebbles in wet clay.

He studiously examined the soles of Skippy's red high-top sneakers. He'd always thought his friend wore such thick soles because it made him look taller, which was funny on account of his being too tall for his weight as it was.

Ben also noticed the baggy Hawaiian shorts which gave the dead boy's skinny legs an even scrawnier appearance. And yet another thought moonwalked through Ben's numbed mind: how interesting it was that he could make out the pattern of the other boy's shorts and even the treads of his high-tops although the feeding was taking place a good five hundred yards away, with the night's only illumination coming courtesy of the ghastly yellow-but-not-yellow moon.

Thing was, Ben spent so much time gawking at Skippy's shoes that he barely noticed the winged toad hovering over his unmoving form. Hovering and occasionally dipping its reddened, oddly beaked mouth.

Maybe he'd have paid the whole scene a lot more attention, but just then someone shouted "Tony!" and even though the voice had changed—had lost a great deal of its authority over the course of the unique evening—Ben knew it was Greg calling out for his brother.

In Ben's desire to return to the petty annoyances of the real world, he heard in Greg's cry the exasperation of a kid just realizing he'd left his homework on the bus. Just like his mind had called the thing eating Skippy a winged toad, a specimen he could almost understand, almost find on a field trip with Mrs. DeVane's science class. After all, the thing did look something like a smaller, sharper-toothed version of the amphibious Lagoon Creature from Sunday afternoon cable. And until you add water, an amphibian is basically a reptile, isn't it? Now, if you just introduce a scabrous, veiny pair of wings to the picture...

Ben had to catch hold of himself, and he knew it. In his haste to retain his sanity, he was converting every critical thought into a safe triviality, and that could kill him. Ben blinked, forced himself to focus on his immediate surroundings.

He saw three other figures hunkered low to the ground, almost lost in the shadows which had draped the remaining landscape ever since the unnatural moonlight had aimed itself like a spotlight at the distant point where the toad creature was feeding upon their friend.

Right away Ben knew that Tony Luckinbill wouldn't be one of those hunkered-down figures. Knew it like he instinctively knew the grade he was getting on a math test he forgot to study for.

Greg called out Tony's name again, this time in a sharper voice. A voice that would have brought his missing brother on the run if he were anywhere nearby. He wasn't.

Greg turned to Ben, his face grim, alien, pale. "Ben, where'd you see him last?"

"On the path," he answered after a moment's thought. "Just after the slime stuff started falling." He ran a hand through his black, knotted hair at the terrible memory.

"He was leading," Danny added. "I thought he brought us here."

Greg jumped up as if bucked by an adrenaline charge. "Come on. We're going back."

Ben couldn't think of anything worse than backtracking, unless it was continuing to sit in that enormous field waiting for the toad to finish its first course. "This is a horrible place," he whispered, stating the obvious.

"Wait," Trevor said. "We can't just leave Skippy."

Trevor had been the only one still looking at the horror where the field rose, and later, on the path, he would tell Ben how the wrinkled creature with the bloodshot wings and the thick, twisted legs had turned when he said that; had turned and looked him straight in the eye and had grinned, and a voice that went straight to the boy's brain, bypassing his ears, had said, *I'll have you for dessert, old Trevor my boy.*

"There's nothing we can do for him, though," Trevor added, second-guessing his initial comment.

No one disagreed.

The first thing Ben found as they retraced their steps was that the path had changed and was straying off of its original course. The trees were squattier here, and joined by even stubbier vegetation: black bushes with thick, pale fruit that Ben had definitely not noticed before. He informed the others about the changes to the terrain.

"Shit," Greg said. "If we're on a different path, we'll never find Tony."

"That's not what I mean," Ben replied glumly. "Same path, different *location*." He didn't like to hear what he was saying, but truth was truth, and it apparently didn't have to resemble reality as they all used to know it.

"That doesn't make sense," Greg muttered, but without much conviction. The evening's festivities had left him without a heated argument against the existence of a footpath that picked up and relocated when it felt like it.

So they kept walking, Ben's tired feet bogging down in the spongy surface. Every once in a while one of them would softly call out for the missing boy, and sometimes they'd get an answer back from the woods that fell off of either side of the path.

Only it wouldn't come from Tony.

Ben tried hard not to listen to these other voices; voices that sounded like wild animals attempting human speech for the first time and having fun with the concept.

"Over here, Ben," he heard once. Only none of the other boys looked up, so maybe it had been merely one sharp branch scraggling another in a breeze he couldn't feel.

He tried not even thinking about those voices that he might not actually be hearing. Paying any attention at all could make him leave that path, and that wasn't something he was particularly interested in doing.

At other times he heard ice cream music far in the distance, but it didn't tempt him to seek the source. At least there was no more slime.

Maybe they walked for hours. Walked and called out Tony's name, but in tones that would have been hard to hear even if the lost boy were just footsteps away. The words had a hard time escaping from such tight, dry throats.

The only thing they had going for them, from Ben's point of view, was that Greg was in charge again. Losing his brother had pulled him most of the way back into his old self. Greg's sense of responsibility was burdening him with a desperation that was stronger than fear. It propelled him on a mission that left no room for failure.

"Tony's here," something croaked in a voice like cracked soil.

They all heard that one.

Then other, weaker voices, less successful at their first attempts at speech, joined in. "Come get little brother, Greg," these creatures might have been saying, although the words weren't at all clear. "He's with us, Greggy."

"Don't do it," Trevor said once when Greg stopped and studied the dark woods too long. "I don't think they can get us if we stay up here."

That was a comforting line of defense, like being able to ward off vampires with homemade crosses and garlic cloves, so they gratefully accepted Trevor's theory. They stayed on the path. They walked. They kept as far from those black trees as possible, and ignored—tried to ignore—the squat bushes loaded down with the sickly, fat fruit swaying in a breeze that Ben still couldn't feel.

Occasionally, the hideous light from above would flicker, and Ben was forced to imagine membranous wings gliding through the starless sky to momentarily block out that foreboding moon. He made a point of never looking up when the yellow light weakened, and neither did the other three.

Then Ben saw it, and at first the sight filled him with hope. He wasn't the only one fooled; they all were. They ran to it, welcoming its return into their lives: the culvert, the storm drain, the tunnel; whatever damned thing it was, they loved it like a grandmother fresh from a tropical cruise, arms bent with gaudy souvenirs.

Ben felt nervous getting off of the path to kneel in front of the opening within the vine-infested hillside, but only a little. He wanted so badly for things to get better, for this gateway to be their ticket home.

"Wait," Trevor ordered. "What if this thing's not...right?"

They stepped back, their fallen expressions proof of how well they understood the potential problem. Ben shuddered. The tunnel wasn't where they'd left it, and surprises in this yellow world tended not to be pleasant.

Finally, he said, "What choice do we have? You guys wanna hang around here any longer?"

"We have to stay," Greg answered. He stared hard at each of the others.

Ben arched his eyebrows like he didn't clearly understand the older boy's words, but he did.

"Listen," Greg said. "I'm not asking anyone to come with me. In fact, it makes more sense for you all to stay here and watch that...hole so it doesn't disappear again. And when I call out, answer me so I can find my way back in case the path takes off again. So just...stay. Okay?"

They said nothing, none of them. Ben stared into the shaft, then glanced ever-so-quickly toward the grasping woods. His gaze caught everything in the immediate vicinity but the eyes of the older Luckinbill.

"He's my *brother*," Greg said, answering a question that no one had raised. He sounded on the verge of tears.

The thought of that made Ben's own throat constrict. He wondered why the death of Skippy hadn't reduced any of them to tears. That, in turn, reminded him of the stony-faced war refugees in those films they showed at school sometimes. Then he understood it in its terrible simplicity: certain situations trivialize tears.

"We'll stay," Danny said.

Ben couldn't keep his mind from replaying footage of the winged toad chewing away at one friend. It didn't make him too hopeful about Tony. "Yeah, we'll stay," he very reluctantly promised.

Trevor said, "I'll go with you, Greg." Then he turned to his best friend and added, "Ben, you and Danny guard the tunnel. We'll be back soon as we can."

Ben never wanted to stop hearing their fading footfalls. At first, he called himself a coward for staying behind while Greg and Trevor trudged back. Then it dawned on him that he was in just as much danger here with Danny, the two of them crouching in front of the tunnel opening. Is it worse to meet danger head-on, or to lag behind with your back exposed? There was no preferable course of action to lead him out of this nightmare he'd stepped into.

So now it was just Danny and him.

The other boy scooted so close that it would have been embarrassing under any other circumstance, but at that particular moment Ben wouldn't have minded his annoying friend sitting in his lap and asking for his hand in marriage. Least it would be a human hand.

"How long should we wait, Ben?"

Danny sounded so uncharacteristically serious that Ben wouldn't have known it was him without the harsh benefit of yellow moonlight.

"Maybe, I don't know...a half-hour?" Ben wished that level-headed Trevor was still around to do the thinking for all of them.

"That, that's a long time, isn't it?"

A half-hour? Not if you spent it swimming at the Mundy Street Pool or playing Nintendo or trading sports cards with Trevor. But right now? Longer than forever. For the first time, Ben began to understand perspective.

He was about to comment along those lines, just to be talking and not thinking, when they both heard Skippy in the bushes.

In those late-night cable movies where the unknown, expendable actors and actresses hear voices like that—voices from their dead friends—they get stupid like they think the whole experience has just been a bad dream and there's really nothing to be afraid of.

But Ben had the sudden insight that it doesn't work that way in real life. He became a fervent and properly terrified believer in the unbelievable from the opening greeting of Skippy in the bushes. From the very first syllables.

"Hey guys, why'd you leave me back there?" Skippy's voice sounded muffled by the black leaves that hid him, but it was definitely his. "Ben? Danny? C'mere, I wanna talk to you guys."

Danny grabbed Ben's hand and held on tight.

"Don't say anything back," Ben whispered.

The bush twitched, a yard or so to the side of the tunnel. "Hey, Ben," the voice whined like only Skippy could whine. "What's going on, you guys? C'mere, huh?"

Again the bush twitched, harder this time.

"You're dead, Skippy," Ben said, disobeying his own order.

The voice in the bush didn't argue that point. Ben was hoping for once that Danny would come up with one of his stupid wisecracks. Something that would take their minds for even a second off of what they were hearing. Instead, his friend kept a very respectful silence.

"It's not so bad," the Skippy-voice finally said. "Being dead, I mean. Try it, Ben. With me."

"No!" he shouted back, scaring both Danny and himself.

The voice chuckled in that drought-choked tone that swallowed humor, the desiccated laughter he'd heard from the woods. "It's gonna happen anyway, goofnuts. I toldcha. I told you all, but no one would listen. Remember? Now I know what the situation is: I'm one of the people who just knows stuff. Premonitions, you know? There's lots of folks like that to one degree or another, only it's usually such a weak talent they don't even know about it. But this place, this place brings it all out, magnifies our powers. It's too cool, you guys."

The bush rattled. "There'll be lots more of us when we make it to the other side. Whatever's gonna happen is gonna happen. So c'mon and get it over with, okay?"

Ben could almost imagine that he was *really* hearing his friend. It would be so easy to believe, to just simply *believe*.

"Maybe he's right," Danny said, his voice cracking. "If we can't do anything else...I just want this scariness to be over."

Ben gripped his living friend as hard as he knew how. "We're not doing anything but wait here for Greg and Trevor. This...Skippy...can't do anything to us as long as we stay put."

Ben didn't know where he got that idea. He was just trying to comfort Danny, but he had himself half-convinced as well.

Until the bush parted and dead Skippy looked out.

Chapter Eighteen

The phone lines were humming in Cleary by evening, the gossipy and curious and frantic calls crisscrossing the town and the nation. Panicky parents became children again as they sobbed out sketchy details to their own parents. Neighbors informed and updated neighbors, trading theories, formulating conspiracies, and augmenting facts with enlightening rumors, some of which were no doubt created right there on the spot.

The lines hummed.

At eleven thirty, Megan Crocker placed a call to Camp Brighton, out near Washington Court House, and demanded to be put in contact with her sleeping daughter.

The silence which took over the line while the voice on the other end went away to comply was the longest on record. She kept imagining the camp counselors huddling nervously together to figure out a way to break the news to Jessie's already concerned mother: *For some reason your little girl can't be located right now, but we're sure it's nothing...*

The woman who'd answered had sounded funny, now that Megan thought about it. Nervous? Confused? Probably nothing more than the expected response to a mother placing a late-night call for her overnighting child. No doubt the counselors had handled the reverse of the situation on countless occasions: frightened campers demanding the voices of understanding mothers. Rarely the other way around, Megan supposed.

And how young that voice on the other end of the line had sounded! Just what were the age requirements for these counselors? Megan had never wondered before, had always implicitly trusted her little girl's safety to faceless, nameless strangers who might not be much older than their charges.

What type of and how much training did these counselors receive? What about their first-aid skills? Where was the nearest hospital, and would the rustic roads into and out of the place readily accommodate an ambulance in a hurry?

Those questions and more drilled away at Megan's skull, chipping gleefully into layers of psyche to expose her maternal failings like raw nerves. She hadn't cared enough to ask the crucial questions when the asking mattered, and that was why—

"Mom, what's the matter?" The ten-year-old sounded lost and frightened in the way that everyone sounds when awakened by telephone.

She was so young, so fragile. What had Thad and she been thinking, sending their little girl away for an entire two weeks alone?

"Nothing, Jess," she answered quickly, her voice achieving a false soprano. She was working too hard to establish her innocence, to convince both her daughter and herself that there had been absolutely no reason for her near-midnight phone call.

Have to survive this, have to survive. That had been her mantra for the last couple hours, while her chest threatened to explode from pent-up pressure.

"I just wanted to hear the sound of your voice, honey bear. Make sure you were all right."

Make sure you weren't dead.

The line went silent, Jessie waiting to hear more, knowing that there had to be more.

"Mom, is everything really okay? You sound, I don't know, different. Like when Grandpa died."

Megan harshly cleared her throat of welling emotion and night panic. Jessie had been all of six when Megan's father had passed away.

93

She had called her two children from the old man's house while the body was still warm, just to convince them that everything was fine. Jessie had known different, had been more perceptive than Ben, yet she'd accepted her grandfather's death with the serenity that Megan herself couldn't feel. Perhaps not even to the present day.

How much do children really know about what goes on around them? Megan suspected that the adult population might feel rather uncomfortable if it were known how easily their children track their lies of speech inflection, body language, eye-contact avoidance.

"It's just that I love you so much," Megan finally said, her chest stoppered with the utter truth of the statement. "And Ben too, of course. Love both of my wonderful kids. Honey, I'm sorry I got you up for this." Then she added, although she could barely force the words past the knot in her throat, "Everything's fine, honey. I promise it is."

A lie, but sometimes only a lie will save your soul.

It was information, not love, that was being shared via yet another phone call that evening. The call had been postponed all day, until it could be put off no longer.

Joanie Danver possessed a bubbliness that could turn to quiet simmer with merely a pause and a thoughtful inhalation. It was that dreaded lull in the conversation that Tom Luckinbill was experiencing. It had followed his interruption of her chatty account of the weekend alone with Evan.

She finally released her breath in an insistent sigh that seemed to signal annoyance rather than terror—but Tom knew the truth.

This was going to be a bad one.

"What do you mean, they're missing?"

It didn't come out like a question; more of a statement that she was expecting him to contradict, to tell her that she'd heard him wrong and of course her two boys weren't missing, they were both safely tucked in for the night.

Speaking as carefully as he knew how, he said, "Things are a little confusing around here right now. Although we don't know where they're at, we're not seriously considering foul play."

Christ, he sounded like a public relations officer trying to snow the press into a false sense of calm. "I just thought you should know," he finished weakly.

There was so much to say, so many follow-up questions. He knew that his ex-wife's silence was only to sort through the numerous possibilities.

When she finally spoke, her voice contained such deadly calm that it was even worse than an emotional outburst. "Tell me," she said. "Tell me everything."

He did. He even admitted to working on his day off, a violation of his promise to her that he'd find time for the boys that weekend. While unveiling the facts for her benefit, he wondered when she'd jump in with her icy accusations.

Her silence was worse. It accumulated as slowly and steadily as frost. He'd pause, actually listening for a sound from the other end, and hear nothing until she asked about the auto show in Dayton.

Sounding less patient than he'd wanted to, he asked her what she was talking about.

"The car show. You know. Greg said they were going to see if you'd take them. When you came up busy today, maybe they got resentful and went with someone else's parent. How'd they sound when you told them you couldn't go?"

Tom was sitting in his office, his desktop somewhere under a new generation of fast-food wrappers, soft drink and coffee containers, and unreturned phone-call slips from worried and outraged residents. His door was closed. It made the tiny office even tinier, but at least it kept out the sounds and smells of his involuntary guests down the corridor.

"They mentioned it, but we agreed to reschedule for another time," he lied. The truth was, he could neither confirm nor deny that such a conversation ever took place. The three of them must have talked about something at breakfast that morning or yesterday, whenever it was they'd last shared a meal. But whatever the details, they were gone now. Simply gone.

"Evan's at the grocery store," Joanie said.

Groceries, Tom thought. What kind of man pushes a shopping cart at damned near midnight?

"When he gets back," she continued, "he'll start making phone calls. I don't know why the Highway Patrol isn't involved yet, but Evan will find out. Come to think of it, I can dial a few numbers myself."

This person used to be his wife. Tom had to keep reminding himself, because he no longer knew her.

Following the separation, Joanie had taken a job in the office of Mark Perry's Oldsmobile dealership, her first full-time position since college. Five months after the divorce came through, she'd packed up the boys and moved fifty miles up the road to the state capital without much in the way of personal belongings or explanation. And less than a year after that, word had nonchalantly filtered back to Tom by way of a son that there was a wedding in the works.

The lucky man was Evan Danver, an attorney for some State House subcommittee. In the course of subsequent and casual interrogations of the boys, it was learned that the purpose of the subcommittee was to oversee the budgets and practices of Ohio's law enforcement agencies. And in case Tom needed more surprises in his life, Joanie had already come aboard as her fiancé's aide. There was to be no explanation of how she had met a man connected with law enforcement if not through Tom, or at various out-of-town seminars at which she had accompanied her former husband.

At any rate, Joanie Luckinbill had disappeared. The woman taking her place was a stranger to Tom, and it had taken him four years to realize it.

"Are you listening to me?" she asked him crisply. "You'll have to give us about two hours to put the word out in Columbus, then to drive down. If you can't get ahold of us here, it'll be because we're on our way. Here's our mobile phone number."

He should have remembered he had valuable state contacts through Joanie and the new husband he'd never met. If anything were to happen that could have been avoided by an earlier phone call, he'd never forgive himself.

"Are you taking this down, Tom? Come on, we don't have time to waste."

Chapter Nineteen

Deputies Kempton and Wade were both tall, young, and neatly mustached. They even blinked together as they stepped out of their Fayette County cruiser, parked on Cleary Center, and waited to receive the town's delegation of two. Tom could see at a glance that each was still in the first stage of a cop's life, when he appreciates his toned body enough to keep pounding it into a warrior mold. Only later would the burgers and steak catch up. Only later would the monotony of exercise be replaced with the regularity of spectator football and participant beer.

"About time," Tom snapped as he marched down to the curb in front of the police station to meet them, Thad trailing behind.

The two, already ramrod straight, managed somehow to stand even taller, "Sorry, Chief Luckinbill," one of them said crisply.

This one was Kempton, if Tom remembered right. He'd run into both men at county functions. Now he couldn't help wondering if either partner had met his ex-wife.

The usually mild-mannered Thad Crocker wanted to know why Sheriff Gattis could only spare a solitary cruiser to make the rounds every few hours. "Don't you know what kind of problems we have here?" he asked. "Or doesn't anyone care?"

Tom could hear Kempton swallow hard. "Sir, me and Deputy Wade here can only follow orders."

"And you've been ordered to damned near ignore us?" Thad shouted.

Tom put a hand on the mayor's forearm. "Easy, Thad," he said. Then, to the deputies, "There are missing children involved, or we wouldn't be so hard on you both." It felt to him like he and Thad had switched their good-cop bad-cop roles.

"Yes, sir," Kempton said. "That's why we came. It's just that our understanding of the situation is that there hasn't been much of an actual emergency. The strangers aren't violent—we've looked into some of their backgrounds, and we know that there's nothing linking any of them to the disappearances in any provable way. So with six boys missing in broad daylight..."

The longer Kempton went without interruption, the more assured he became. For good reason: the words made sense.

"...and your department assuming primary responsibility, Sheriff Gattis didn't see cause for intervention. It's only now, with nightfall and the kids' whereabouts still unknown that..."

Tom waved the deputy's speech to a conclusion. "Yeah, we know," he said. "We're just wound pretty tight, that's all."

Kempton's posture loosened almost imperceptibly. "That's understandable, sir."

"No shit," Wade said, speaking for the first time. His voice was higher than his partner's, higher than his physique should have allowed. "Especially with that maniac Durwood roaming your town."

"He's not roaming, he's locked up," Tom said tersely.

"Still..." the second deputy replied, letting the full impact of his thoughts go unspoken.

Nice bedside manner, Tom thought. Kempton at least had the decency to look uncomfortable on behalf of his partner.

Thad stuck an elbow in Tom's ribs and nodded toward the street.

First he saw one, then two, three...

"New arrivals," Thad muttered.

The two deputies turned to see tattered shadows poking from behind the abandoned Kinston Mansion that had last served as the town's museum.

In one of their few idle conversations of the past, Thad Crocker had explained the concept of Edge Cities to Tom. They were unplanned metropolitan areas that sprang up and away from the centers of major cities as businesses and individuals fled crime, pollution, overpopulation, and other urban blights. The phenomenon was associated with large metropolitan areas, but both Thad and Tom had seen it happen in their own small town as commerce crept toward Route 35, which streamed toward Interstate 71 and the choice of Columbus or Cincinnati. They'd watched the minimum-wage food retailers, the cookie-cutter discount stores, and the one-size-fits-all shopping malls misdirect shoppers away from the late-nineteenth-century Victorian shops at the heart of the modest downtown.

The resulting depopulated streets and buildings lent a haunting quality to the nighttime scene that was outlined in yellow by a few old-fashioned mercury vapor lights on gray metal poles.

"Who are they?" Kempton asked.

Under the slightest breeze, Tom could detect the city smell of crowded buses on a hot day. *Dad, we're coming for you.*

Tom stepped back, blinked, watched the solemn but unchanged expressions on the faces of the deputies and the mayor.

"What's the matter?" Thad asked.

Tom listened. "Did you hear…?"

Only the wind. And teenage laughter.

Coming, Dad…

It was directionless, the voice. Like Tom was on the wrong end, hearing it inside-out. The longer and harder he listened, the more transparent it became, until it slipped away to nothing, like the surreal experience of trying to retain a groggy dream upon awakening.

Tom emptied his lungs slowly and returned his attention to the night. Too much work, too much tension, no sleep.

The ragged people shuffled away from the cruiser and police authority, disappearing into the shadows to wait elsewhere.

Wait for what?

"Hell, I'm just glad Albert Durwood's in your town and not mine," Wade said with a high, nervous chuckle.

Chapter Twenty

What's wrong with this picture? Just ten minutes before, Steve Addams had been sitting in his own damned kitchen, drinking his own damned beer and minding his own damned business. Just like things should be, this supposedly being a vacation day to be spent with his new and none-too-understanding wife Chrissie.

So here's the problem, he thought: Vern Withers pulling his squad car up to the Addams' family driveway, stomping out and interrupting Steve's end-of-work routine with his ugly and ill-tempered presence.

The real tragedy of the thing was that the obnoxious and overbearing cop's midnight presence was courtesy of Steve Addams himself, so he had absolutely no one else to blame.

Steve hurried out so as to keep the older man's outbursts to a minimum volume and duration.

"So what's this all about?" Vern growled.

"Keep it down, will you? This street's full of sleeping kids."

"My heart bleeds." Vern Withers leaned against their beat-up Ford squad car and crossed his stumpy arms. "Okay," he said in a stage whisper guaranteed to draw more attention than a shout. "So we finally go off duty after the longest stint in our lives, and now when I should be comfortably drinking at home, you call me back without a word's explanation. What gives?"

Steve leaned against the cruiser. Just leaned and stared the older cop down.

"Aw shit," Vern muttered.

"Not so loud."

"You wanna go back to the park."

"I'm not any happier about it than you are. But weird as it sounds—"

"One of many words that come to mind."

"I saw what I saw," Steve said for about the tenth time that evening.

Vern Withers scraped the back of his neck with a calloused palm. "You ever try living with my Laura. May and missing dinner because you're pulling a double shift?"

"Can't say that I have."

"How about sneaking out of the house at nearly midnight with the world's most lame-brained excuse: my partner needs me?"

"Never tried that one either. Too obvious."

"Well, I've done both those things today. I'm probably going to go home and find out I'm not married anymore, thanks a lot. And all because you want me to help you find some kids been swallowed up by the earth."

Steve could think of worse fates than not being married to Laura May Withers, but he kept the thought to himself. "You can thank me properly later. But I saw what—"

"I know; I know. Just don't tell me again."

"Will you come with me?"

Vern turned away and stepped into the car. "Get in," he muttered. "We're off to see the wizard."

Chapter Twenty-One

Yellow moonlight had caught Skippy's dead face and not let go. He—it—had a crawly, colorless look that was marred further by black, expressionless eyes.

Skippy didn't step out of the bush. He just stared at Danny and Ben, grinning. Propped up against razor-sharp black leaves, unreal.

As much as the sight of dead Skippy terrorized Ben, it was nothing compared to the looks of the fat, pale fruit pulling on the bush. He'd noticed the fruit earlier, in the woods, but hadn't paid enough attention.

Danny also saw them, which was the reason he grabbed Ben around the neck like he was trying to attach himself. The boys didn't scream. Didn't run. Just held on.

It wasn't actually fruit at all. Faces. Little withered faces, miniatures with tiny features all screwed up in horror and loss. Several little mouths twisted into petite ovals like silent screams. Pink kitten-tongues lounged on chins the size of acorns.

Then Ben knew why Skippy didn't leave that bush. He was being sucked up into it, as if nature's ripening process was stuck on Rewind. Soon there'd be nothing left but a tiny round head with a miniature *O* of pain and torment.

"Danny. Ben. Go." It was Trevor.

They'd been so taken by dead Skippy peeking out of the bush that the boys hadn't heard Trevor running up the path, his footfalls silently sucking at the corky surface. Now he long-jumped from the path to land in a squat position next to his friends.

Trevor held out his arm like Vanna White, only he was pointing out the culvert and there wasn't a game-show smile on his face. Not even close.

"Where's Greg?" Ben asked. "And Tony?"

"Don't know," Trevor answered, gasping for breath. "But we can't hang around here any longer. Move it."

"Trevor, there's something—" Ben looked at the bush. It was still twitching a little, but dead Skippy was gone and the yellow moonlight wasn't shining on it like before. Mercifully, he couldn't see the tiny heads. "Never mind. What happened to you guys?"

"No time," Trevor hissed. "I'll tell you on the other side."

Danny let go of Ben. "I want outta here," he said.

Ben looked back and saw someone coming their way from where Trevor had come. "Wait a minute. Maybe it's Greg."

The someone came closer. Just a dark shadow in the strange moonlight. Shouldn't have been dark, though, with all that light spilling on it.

Then Ben saw that the thing would have looked that way even at high noon in a well-lit room. It was black and featureless, but a different shade of black than the surrounding landscape. It was big and tall and its arms were too long and its neck too short.

Ice cream music tinkled merrily in the distance.

"*Get in there,*" Trevor screamed, dragging his friends after him into the tunnel.

Danny was sobbing, calling for his mother. The tunnel glistened. And it *moved.* Just a little, in and out like lungs. Ben tried crawling through without using his hands, but couldn't. His stomach sent acid to his throat as he rubbed against the warm, soft sides. The tunnel smelled like blood, Ben thought, though he couldn't actually remember ever having smelled blood before.

"Ben, I can't. It's...swallowing us," Danny cried.

"Don't turn back," Ben shouted from behind Danny.

Trevor started swearing, threatening his friends with all sorts of wild, bad things if they didn't follow. His voice should have echoed, but didn't. It was nearly lost in that dark, gutsy moistness.

Ben closed his eyes, made himself crawl on. He was sweating in the stifling, humid air. It stung wherever he'd long ago ripped snot creatures from his body. His unprotected back trembled when he imagined the dark thing on the path sneaking into the tunnel to grab him. He begged Trevor to tell him they were getting closer.

"We're almost there."

"What if they're following? What if those things are right behind me now?" Danny sounded almost giddy with panic.

"*I'm* behind you," Ben shouted.

"*Just keep going.*"

Ben had never heard Trevor sound so loud and dangerous before. He tried to quit imagining what his friend had seen back there with Greg.

The thought of Greg...and Tony and Skippy...it made him want to lie down and quit, all that sadness. They'd been his friends for most of his life. Leaving them behind felt like a depth of atrocity his conscience could only begin to fathom.

But anyone else would have done the same if they'd seen those horrors in the...

Moonlight.

Ben had never felt so good about seeing it—the regular moon—in his whole life.

"What is it?" Danny asked. As if he'd forgotten what the real thing looked like.

It wasn't actually the moon, Ben noticed as the three closely examined the tunnel opening. It was better. Common, sweet, man-made American streetlight.

The tunnel hadn't come out exactly where they'd crawled into it, but pretty close. They were on Becker Street, at the north end of their baseball field. Ben recognized every normal detail: the Latkowskis' pink house; Barry Miller's folks' new Geo Tracker, the FOR SALE sign in front of the blind lady's place.

That's how *right* everything was.

They stayed frozen in hunched position, the head of one nervous boy shoved under an armpit or squeezed against a shoulder of another, all wedged in so tight together as to be one creature with excess parts. All too chillingly reminiscent of the demented land they'd left behind. They sniffed the air like mice in a secure crevice, Ben wondering whether they could venture out. He stared into a safe world of normal stars and a normal moon and normal trees they'd climbed but never really noticed until now.

"Let's go," Danny said, nudging Trevor forward. His face was tear-and-dirt-stained. "I just wanna go home. I'm real late, probably in a whole lot of trouble."

Trevor didn't move from the tunnel opening, making Ben nervous all over again.

"See anything, Trev? Anything bad?"

His best friend turned and smiled. "No. It's okay. I'm just shaky, still. Go on ahead."

Trevor stepped aside so Ben and Danny could pass, then let Ben pull him out of the tunnel. "Thanks, Ben," Trevor said, a strange smile on his face. Ben nodded, wondering what additional horrors his friend had seen. But the thoughts fled his mind as he smelled the air and his feet hit planet Earth. He actually started to laugh a little.

"What are you, crazy?"

Danny sounded so angry that it made Ben laugh even harder. "Yeah, I guess I am," he chortled.

"I just wanna go home," Danny said. "Before I get in trouble."

"Me too," Ben said, doubling over with uncontrollable laughter. "We wouldn't want to get in any trouble, now would we, Trevor? Trevor, how are we going to explain—?"

Ben looked back and the next word out of his mouth was "Go," only now he was talking to Danny, definitely not to Trevor.

Danny also turned, and started whimpering something that sounded like, "Oh God oh God don't let it get me."

Like it had gotten Trevor.

Danny and Ben were running hard, panting hard as they raced down silent Becker Street, athletic shoes flapping against pavement.

Someone shouted "Hey, stop!" from back by the tunnel, and that drove them even harder, faster down the wide street, past houses with large, lit porches; houses and porches that should have made Ben feel warm and safe, but didn't. There was no warmth or safety to be found. Only Ben's survival instinct kept him going.

The monster was splitting out of the Trevor mask, or else—an even more terrifying thought—it had been Trevor all along. Ben never did know for sure, but he was sure of this much: Danny and he—okay, mostly he—had let the terrible thing in. It needed someone to issue the invitation and clear a path, and Ben had gone so far as to pull the monstrosity forever into their lives.

Ben also knew that they'd let in more than just the hairy thing with two heads, Trevor's and its own rotting, wormy, blood-clogged one. Worse than that even, they'd ushered in yellow moonlight.

Again he heard the ice cream truck, only now it was so close that the gentle hum of a well-tuned engine accompanied the nostalgic childhood melodies.

Chapter Twenty-Two

"Hey, stop!" Steve Addams shouted.

The boys kept running.

"Who were they?" Steve asked. "One of them looked like the Crocker kid, didn't it?"

They hadn't found the boys where Steve was sure he had seen them disappear earlier, but they'd cruised the Waylock Park area for only a few minutes before spotting them on Becker Street. Spotted them through the curious glow that was beginning to coat the darkness.

Vern Withers didn't answer. He wasn't even looking in the direction of the two boys still pounding pavement. He was watching the tunnel.

"Come on Vern, we've got to..." Steve's words faded to nothing once he tracked his partner's gaze and saw the third figure, the one who hadn't taken off at a dead run with the other two boys. It remained standing by the culvert, wrapped in that strange light that seemed to be escaping the tunnel like a feeble and alien sunbeam.

"Jesus." If Vern Withers managed to say more, it was drowned out by the sound of snapping flesh as the two-headed boy-beast stretched and grew. Old skin shattered and fell away to make room for the tough, leathery flesh now being exposed for the first time.

One head, the one with a boy's face, shriveled and hardened until it was just an empty husk, something useless to be swept by the slight after-midnight breeze.

Vern Withers took a step forward.

"Easy," Steve warned softly.

His partner took another step, slow and careful, like a high school boy about to pin his first corsage. His eyes never left his date-from-hell.

The thing raised an arm, pointed it skyward.

Steve watched the arm stretch, becoming both thinner and longer. He watched the tunnel, where the glow of a substance resembling both light and mist began to reach for the sky.

"Stay back," he said. He saw something else, thought he saw something else, but couldn't have. It looked like an entire truck, brilliant white with pastel art on a side panel, had just driven out of the four-foot tunnel opening and was following the boys down Becker Street. It tinkled a pleasant version of "Three Blind Mice" as it chugged out of view.

Steve thought about the way dogs are not drawn to television or mirror images because they can't smell the objects they see, so they don't believe their eyes. Similarly, he never saw the ice cream truck climbing out of that Alice-in-Wonderland hole. His mind merely observed the phenomenon without even momentary acceptance.

Vern stopped. He unsnapped his holster flap.

The creature saw the older cop as if for the first time. Its stretching arm reached a good six feet beyond the top of its head before descending at a blurring speed to swat the cop aside.

Steve heard bones break. Skull bones. Face bones. His partner went down.

The creature turned toward Steve. The blackened arm, impossibly long even for the still-growing body, took a backhand slap at the surviving cop. The aim was worse this time, the arm whizzing past him like a brushback fastball. It left a heavy smell in the air. Like charcoal, but more pungent.

Steve Addams backpedaled, fighting for balance on the crabby surface. Cleary hadn't seen rain for days, and the park grounds were pitted with crusted soil like moon turf. But now it seemed too bouncy, as alien to the touch as the thing before him was to the eye.

He grabbed his gun and pulled it from his holster, an action he'd never taken anywhere but at a target range. Aimed. It was hard to see the monster under the weird light. It made the creature glow, made it seem to float his way.

He took a two-handed Dirty Harry stance, feet planted firmly. Squeezed the trigger six times, then several times more on empty cylinders until his befuddled mind could bring his itchy finger back under control.

The thing went down, damned right, no doubt about it. The .38 nearly cut the bastard in two, this being no drive-in horror flick where the monster keeps coming when the poor son-of-a-bitch cop runs out of bullets. No fucking way. This was real life where you shoot something from ten, twelve feet, it goes down and doesn't get up again. Not even a twitch, end of story.

Steve lowered his gun. Holstered it. Took one look at his partner and figured there was no rush for an ambulance. Vern Withers's head looked as pulpy as a jack-o'-lantern well into November.

Okay, Steve thought. There was a procedure to follow here, and if he could just remember it, he could begin to get his life and the evening back on firm ground. Okay. Partner's down, assailant's down, strange light's growing stronger...*okay*. Just handle it, Steve ole boy. Just handle it and ignore the way your heart's hammering and stomach's pumping acid like a testy volcano. Pay no attention to your strong inclination to just roll over in bed and hide under your pillow and get at least a few hours of nightmare-free sleep. Pay no attention because this is real life and if you want to stay in the ballgame, you gotta remember that, pal.

Something moved. The monster corpse twitched. Steve backed away and watched squirming pink bodies emerge from the dead thing's ripped chest and stumble into the horrible moonlight.

Hairless fetuses with snouts and tiny, drooling mouths. Six of them. Eight. Maybe ten, but who's counting?

Steve heard rustling sounds like a really large snake might make shedding dead skin. *Really* large snake.

The infant grotesques popped out of the corpse covered with a thick green coating of afterbirth and shredded chest cavity. Steve *thought* the things were green, but colors were indefinite under the strange light in the hazy atmosphere. Even the grass looked different, stiff and faintly glowing. Steve could see the outline of every single blade, the colors all washed together.

The pink creatures saw him, rushed him. They ran on two short legs, but sideways, something in their movements making Steve think of raccoons. Didn't think much though; no time.

The first one sank a set of needle-teeth into his leg just below the knee, as high as the thing could reach.

Another jumped from a half-dozen feet away and slashed through his shirt, opening up a shallow but long chest wound.

A third sank tiny claws into an ankle.

Steve swatted at the one on his chest. It lost its grip but took skin as it fell. It squirmed helplessly on its back, trying to right itself. Steve raised his foot, a pink monstrosity still clinging to it, sucking, nursing for ankle blood. Sobbing with pain as needle-thin, needle-sharp teeth drilled for bone, he drew the foot back with the little monster still attached, and place-kicked the one on its back. Both monstrosities exploded upon impact. Dropped two of the fuckers in one motion. *Okay.*

He slammed a fist into the pig face of the one who'd bitten his leg, nearly obliterating its only-a-mother-could-love features. Its ruined cranium expelled the stink of motor oil and old fish.

Still they came. Teeth snapped, claws slashed, pinched, gouged. Steve kicked, punched, spun and snarled. They kept coming, kept dying. It didn't take much to waste the things, turn them to alien goo, but there were so many.

He found the cruiser door handle behind him with one exploring, blood-slicked hand, opened it, and flung himself into the passenger seat. One of the little creatures wedged its head in after him, and Steve turned the door into a guillotine.

Plop. *Okay.*

He stabbed the lock button before letting his eyes scan the windshield. No more than three or four of them were still moving.

One slithered into closer view. It clung to the windshield and stared in, its large eyes covered by veiny lids as thin and tough as lizard membrane. It sniffed the air with a nose that was nothing more than a double slit in its bulbous pink head. This one was male, its penis dangling at eye level, smearing the glass with cloudy fluid.

Through the flaring nostrils Steve thought he could see the creature's brain, or what passed for one, pumping, throbbing. Do brains throb? It was too much.

He closed his eyes and tried to slow his heartbeat to something manageable. He pictured Chrissie, his wife, his anchor to reality. If he really had a wife, and her name really was Chrissie, and she really looked the way his mind saw her, then he—Steve Addams of 1213 Garden View, Cleary, Ohio—was not crazy not crazy not crazy.

It was a fluke, his being in Cleary at all. Seven months ago—last damn football season ago, for God's sake— they'd been rooting for the Packers, the home team when you live in Milwaukee, Wisconsin. He had a good enough job writing speeding tickets for rich kids in a nice, stodgy, safe suburb undiscovered by bad guys, to say nothing of monsters. Then Chrissie came home to the apartment saying you're not going to believe this, I got accepted at the law school at Ohio State. So Steve went job hunting, one of the few young cops in America who didn't want to see any action, didn't want to crash dope pads or deal with Uzis or drive-bys or pissed-off psycho postal workers. Just wanted to write tickets to sullen rich kids and give directions to out-of-towners and teach second-graders how to watch out for perverts they'll never meet. So he looked real hard for a job in towns that were nearby but not too nearby—the smaller and duller and farther from big-city Columbus and Dayton and Cincinnati the better—and got hired in safe, dull, routine Cleary, Ohio.

And lived happily ever after.

When he opened his eyes again, the creature had vanished from his windshield. He saw two of them now, backs turned to the cruiser.

They were twitching the same way the thing that killed Vern Withers had twitched.

Steve watched them grow, his hand petting the Remington pump braced between the driver's and passenger's seats. With almost listless curiosity, he wondered if it was even loaded.

They grew and changed, the two remaining monstrosities, but never assumed the elasticity or proportions of the monster who'd posthumously birthed them. Got less than half as big, he'd guess. Steve watched their pink flesh darkening, features developing, maturing. He saw dark scalp hair sprout from nowhere, and other changes. Their genitals withdrew like worms into holes as darkening groins took on the texture and colors of boys' running shorts. T-shirts appeared and clung to torsos, emblazoned with the bold brand logos of the latest and most fashionable athletic apparel. Their feet, at first cloven but now human, reformed into the disguise of scuffed sneakers.

The boys looked back to smile briefly at the bleeding officer—one of the alien bastards even waved—before walking away. They sniffed the air, possibly for the lingering scent of the terrified boys who'd fled the scene before them.

Steve Addams needed sleep, a long nap. He closed his eyes but immediately forced them open. If he slept, he died. There was still enough blood in his system for him to know that simple truth.

He kept wiping fresh blood from his palms onto his pant legs. Didn't know exactly where it all came from, didn't want to know. Nothing hurt, but that must be because his sensation circuits were overloaded. He reached for the radio and pressed a button.

"Car four," he said. "Jeff, you out there?"

Blood dripped onto the call button cradled against his damp chest. Everything hurt. He examined almost rationally the possibility that he would die.

A woman responded. "You got me, Steve. Jeff left just a minute ago to take Kerri Upshaw home. What's up?"

Steve shifted uncomfortably in his cramped position. He was talking to one of the town's part-time dispatchers. For a second he couldn't remember her name. Why was that? He used to date her before she married what's-his-name. Then the memory returned.

"Ellen, this is a ten-three," he croaked. *Officers need help.* His weak voice terrified him. "I'm on Becker Street adjoining the back entrance to Waylock Park. Two officers down. Also, I think a couple of the kids are heading home, probably to the Crocker place. Better send someone to meet them. Someone well armed."

There was a moment's silence as the radio seemed to ponder his words. "Ten four," the dispatcher said, her voice calm and professional. "Hold on, Steve. I'm crazy with calls right now and it's gonna be tough finding units to respond, but you're Priority One."

"The kids," he said. "Help the kids." His numb fingers could no longer tell him if the mike call button was depressed.

Someone rapped on the passenger window.

Steve jumped, sending flares of new pain shivering up and down his body. He huddled as far from the window as possible.

It was Vern Withers. He didn't look good—half his face was caved in and caked with drying blood—but it was definitely his old partner, and Steve was never so glad to see someone in his whole life. One gray moth perched on a knuckle of the hand the cop leaned against the window.

Sure it looked like his old partner had bought the farm back there. Steve had been sure of it at one time, but how could he disbelieve what his glassy eyes now saw?

He leaned over, lifted the lock button, and climbed over into the driver's seat so good old partner Vern could squeeze in next to him.

"My God," Steve said. "Don't worry, I'll get you to a hospital. I thought for sure you were—"

Vern grabbed hold of the younger man's shirt and pulled him forward until they cracked heads together. Then he sank his teeth into Steve Addams's neck, found the jugular, and washed the interior of the cruiser in black blood.

He opened the driver's door and shoved his dying partner out, still twitching like a fish out of water.

Steve Addams's last confused thoughts concerned those dogs on his mind earlier—the ones who don't believe what they see if they can't convince the sense they trust most.

The Vern-thing started the engine and drove away.

Chapter Twenty-Three

The mustached deputy stepped gingerly back into the Fayette County cruiser without spilling too much from the flimsy paper tray he was trying to balance on his lap. "I miss anything?" Wade asked.

"Yeah. Dispatch says 35's crawling with ragged folks, all heading this way. New ones. Even 71's packed like it's some laid-back country road. Guess our people are picking up jaywalkers by the paddywagonload."

As he pulled out of the Burger King lot, Kempton added, "Hey, I wanted a *double* cheeseburger."

"Should have got it yourself."

"Should have stopped at a drive-through like I suggested in the first place. It's Russian roulette when I let you order."

"Nothing open after midnight. Take what you can get. Think Chief What's-his-name'll like us county guys better once he knows we're pulling overtime?"

"How about my coffee? At least you remembered that, didn't you?"

"Just keep your eyes on the road. I'll fix it. Cream?"

"Two creams," Kempton replied. "Two sugars."

"Jesus, you still got a single original tooth in your head?"

"So they don't think we're doing enough, and I understand that," Kempton said. "But we're just following orders. It's not exactly in the county budget to invade this town, come in with guns blazing, tanks rumbling down Cleary Center."

"So you explained. Way you set down the facts to Luckinbill and the mayor...you got a talent for telling people to go to hell in such a way that they thank you and start to pack."

Kempton finished his burger and carefully wiped his lips. "The locals can handle the truth. Anyway, it wasn't me bragging about how lucky I was I didn't live here."

Wade shrugged. "If you can tell the truth, I can tell the truth. Long as Albert Durwood's parked in that flimsy little jail of theirs, home values are falling. Know what I mean?"

After a short silence, Wade said, "Luckinbill's not gonna bitch to Gattis about us being a couple argumentative smartasses, is he?"

"Nah, he's an all right guy most the time. It'd help if we could find those missing kids, of course. Might make the mayor brighten up, too."

"He's one stiff asshole, huh? Crocker, I mean."

Kempton said, "You gotta see things his way. Kid's gone, murderers and junkies and God-knows-what are taking over his town. But if you don't count today, he actually breaks down and smiles on occasion. Or so I'm told. Guess his old man was mayor like forever, and folks tend to compare father to son. Makes him a bit uneasy under pressure. Oh, by the way, one other piece of news while you were out misordering my order. Three more county vehicles are on the way, and it looks like Highway Patrol's finally kicking into action too. Guess someone in Columbus started to squawk."

"Great," Wade said. "Here, drink your coffee. Hey, who's that?"

"Who?"

"Car up ahead."

"Don't know. Looks like a Cleary unit."

"So why's he riding the center line like that? What is he, drunk?"

"Looks like Vern Withers. Don't know why he'd be driving like that, though."

"Rash your lights, man. Son of a bitch, he's drifting our way."

"Holy shit, he's still—"

"Turn, *turn*—"

"Brace yourself. Oh, God, we're gonna—"

Chapter Twenty-Four

"I appreciate your giving me a ride home," Kerri Upshaw said. "But you know I could have driven."

Jeff Smith shrugged as he studied the road ahead. "Lots of wackos out tonight. I wouldn't feel right about it if I'd let you go alone. Anyway, I'm headed home myself, catch a quick nap. It's no problem."

"And I'm a mere four miles out of your way."

Jeff grinned. "More or less."

She squinted at him, tapped the glove box once and returned her attention to the passenger window. "You're a good cop, Officer Smith," she said.

Jeff nodded once, punched in his cigarette lighter. He didn't smoke, but always had a hot lighter: nervous habit. "Thank you." It didn't seem to be a thorough enough response, but he was wary, half-expecting her to offset her brief praise with fresh criticism.

"I know I'm not easy," she said in a low voice. "Maybe it's the kind of day we're having, Jeff. I spent too much of it at city hall trying to comfort parents who, between you and me, might never see their kids again."

"It most likely won't come to that," he offered meekly.

She twitched her head. Whether or not that constituted disagreement was not clear. "Anyway, with all that's happened and is still happening, I just want you to know how much I appreciate your work."

His radio squawked, a welcome distraction. A female voice said, "Code ten three, all units. Two officers down, Becker Street near

Waylock Park. Respond immediately. We also need help at the mayor's residence, 618 Merryside Drive."

Jesus Christ. Jeff actually had his choice of emergencies. Now that was something he wasn't used to. He glanced in his rearview mirror, gently pressed his brake pedal and turned the wheel.

"Come on," Kerri asked. "Let's respond. Don't ignore it just because you're with me. I can handle myself."

"I'm trying," Jeff said grimly. His foot ineffectively pumped the brake.

"What is it?" The town manager sounded ready for anything.

Jeff shook his head. The car's suspension felt funny. Mushy and springy like cork, so that his car kept slogging down and popping back up with a cushiony sensation that seemed unlikely to disturb the shocks.

When he was a kid he'd loved driving the amusement park antique cars, actually fooling himself into believing it was he who controlled the vehicle, not the deeply grooved road. It wasn't until years later that he figured out that his steering wheel didn't do a damned thing but look good.

That's how it was now. The wheel turned, the accelerator worked—he could hear his engine gun when he floored it—but nothing happened. The road was driving, tires wallowing in spongy pavement.

And nothing out his windshield looked right. The colors were all wrong, a mist of some kind settling down around them even as he watched.

"Look," Kerri said.

Their cruiser hopped a curb and abruptly exited Bridge, the street they'd been traveling. They were now paralleling it, juttering down a crude sort of road that had never before existed. A road that looked as though it was being constructed mere seconds ahead of their tires.

Through his rearview mirror he could see another Cleary cruiser coming fast down Bridge, approaching the patch of road they'd traveled seconds before.

"Turn on your emergencies," Kerri ordered.

Jeff flicked the dome switch and added a siren to draw the attention of the other driver. "It's Steve or Vern," he said, recognizing the vehicle. "Don't know why they're not responding."

The Withers/Addams car was straddling the center line, heading toward an oncoming cruiser on Bridge. Jeff, a reluctant spectator, could barely make out FAYETTE COUNTY SHERIFF'S DEPARTMENT on the passenger door of this second car as his own cruiser continued to involuntarily flee the scene. The county cruiser swerved, then swerved again. Each time, Steve and Vern's car mirrored the action.

"What the hell's he doing?" Jeff murmured. His own unit was slowing as if whoever or whatever controlled it was insisting that they hang around to watch the imminent disaster.

Kerri braced herself on one elbow, her body twisted to peer through the back window. "I don't like this," she said.

Jeff had never heard the town manager sound frightened before. What he was seeing had a similar effect on him.

The county car braked hard, fishtailed. Vern or Steve—whoever was driving—kept coming, kept coming.

"Look out!" Kerri shouted ineffectually.

Jeff closed his eyes, ducked instinctively as tearing metal and a sound like thunder—but louder, much louder—ripped open the night.

"Shit." He could feel the reverberation of the collision coursing through his whole body, even his teeth. He was blinded by the white flash of at least one ruptured fuel tank, his face instantly flushed as if with too much Florida sun.

His car—obviously no longer his own—veered sharply as the new road turned farther away from the accident scene, away from the center of town. The road seemed to have been designed by an engineer with a bizarre sense of humor. They passed dangerously close to a Pizza Hut and a Taco Bell on Route 35 before cutting across backyards, even plowing through flimsy privacy fences, scattering teenagers and dogs.

It was a June weekend, and all the locals were out on front porches and in convenience store parking lots. The patrol car's bizarre handling gave the townies something to remember: burning rubber, spitting gravel; not to mention the fireball in the distance.

"It's not happening," Jeff said.

"The fuck it isn't," Kerri snapped.

By now they were in the scrubland outskirts of town. Jeff rubbed his eyes clean of all but a few remaining sun spots from the head-on explosion. He picked up his radio mike, pressed the button and spoke. "Ellen, it's Jeff. I've got a code ten three of my own. Kerri Upshaw and I are heading out by 35 and Crenmore Creek somewhere, I think. Car's out of control, I can't—"

"Jeff, look."

The flat tone of Kerri's voice silenced him. He stared straight ahead, like she was doing. There was nothing but squelch on the police band.

It was a bush planted directly in their path. They watched it poke from the corky soil like a gopher smelling the air, and pull itself up to a height of about four feet in the dead center of the impossible road. Its long, sharp leaves seemed to beckon the car forward. Overripe fruit peeked through the long limbs like—

Jeff and Kerrie covered their faces as the bush plunged two staked limbs through the windshield, but faces weren't what it was after. It rammed their chests and plunked them, skewered and twitching, through the exploding glass.

Chapter Twenty-Five

All right, so think...

Her birthday wasn't for another seven months, and only a real procrastinator would be playing an April fool's trick this late in the year. Besides, she admitted with a puzzled frown, neither Tom Luckinbill nor anyone who wanted to stay employed by the serious police chief would ever pull a prank like this.

So either everything that she'd been through in the last several minutes was some kind of an emergency preparedness drill or...it was real.

The phone rang. Again. Ellen Cooney picked it up and listened.

"We know, ma'am," she managed to say as soon as old Mrs. Worth paused for breath. Ellen wondered—couldn't help it, despite all her other concerns—if the elderly caller knew she was talking to little Ellen Ruhlman, her former next-door neighbor and frequent Saturday-night baby sitter.

"Yes, Mrs. Worth, we know there's been a car accident," Ellen said, squeezing into a tight verbal opening in the excitable woman's chatter. "We're in the process of—"

The dispatcher listened, then nodded, though no one could see the response except maybe the mayor and his wife, still somewhere in the building. "Yes. Uh-huh. Yes, we know the accident involved police cars. Several people have reported...yes...yes. Mrs. Worth, there's help on the way if you'll just—"

At first, Ellen Ruhlman Cooney had been positive she was being tested. Jeff had left the station with town manager Kerri Upshaw practically the moment Ellen clocked in. He'd paused only long enough to tell her that the night could be strange and he'd be back shortly and she'd better hang close to the phone and radio and keep her ears open for anything having to do with six missing boys, and Tom would fill in the details, and by the way, there are thirty or forty blabbering prisoners in the cells down the hall.

Prisoners? Missing boys? Not to mention the shitload of crazies walking the streets. Everyone was talking about them.

So first thing, she gets a ten three—very, *very* weird— from Steve Addams. God, if only she'd snatched him up when she'd had the chance. Anyway, Steve needs immediate back-up, officers down, the whole nine yards just like on TV. Oh, yeah, and send a car to the mayor's residence if you get a chance. His kid's been found.

Uh-huh. So she raises Baylog and Fleming on account of their being the nearest unit available, and meanwhile, Tom Stoneface Luckinbill's standing right behind her—checking out her response procedures, no doubt— and he tells her he'll answer the call to the Crocker residence himself, and don't tell the kid's parents because it'll only upset them if it's a false sighting. And he leaves without the full explanation that Jeff Smith promised she'd get from the chief.

Okay, so far it sounds like a drill, all these split-second decisions, all handled very well by the way, Ellen Ruhlman Cooney. And now she's alone except for the Crockers, who she'd found pacing the break room as she punched in. The phones are ringing off the hooks, all the calls like the one from Mrs. Worth: eyewitness sighting, two police cars, head-on, boom. So this is the point where Ellen starts to doubt her initial theory. The whole town can't be in on this emergency preparedness drill thing, can it? Like they hired a few dozen out-of-work actors to wander the streets like zombies just for effect.

"Uh, yes, Mrs. Worth. We really are taking care of things, and as soon as you hang up..."

And exactly as the phone rings for the eleventh time, her radio crackles again and this time it's Jeff Smith, also cute in his own pleasant way, but without the full head of hair of a Steve Addams.

Jeff's call, even stranger than the others. Another ten three *officer needs help* alarm, cruiser's out of control, blah blah blah, then nothing. Dead air.

And all the while she can hear this background, low-level cackling, like relaxed geese, coming from the incarcerated mob on the other side of the cell corridor door.

"Mrs. Worth, I'm going to have to keep this line open, so if you'd just—"

The front door rattled and heavy footsteps pushed through even as the switchboard light lit to indicate yet another caller. Ellen Cooney felt like the world's most popular midnight radio call-in hostess

She hoped it was Tom or Jeff returning; her back was to the door and she was too damned busy to turn, but sure as hell didn't need to be bothered by any civilian about now.

She stabbed another frantically blinking button. "Cleary Police Department," she said, sounding extra professional in the event that it was Tom Luckinbill slowly making his way toward her.

Another nervous caller...

"Yes, Mr. Roderick, we're aware of the accident and there should be a unit on the scene very shortly..."

Why hadn't someone gotten there already? She'd called Metro for an ambulance and had alerted Tom. What was going on in boring little Cleary, Ohio, tonight?

And what smelled like burnt meat?

"Yes, Mr. Roderick, thank you for the call. Good night, now."

Someone tapped her.

She turned. Dropped the phone. Heard Dale Roderick, her old junior high history teacher (Ellen Ruhlman Cooney, this is your life) still chattering away in his usual roundabout manner, the chatter now coming from somewhere near the floorboards by way of the hastily abandoned telephone.

"Okay, Vern," she said tightly as she began to anchor herself against the waves of revulsion battering her. This was certainly no drill.

"We'll get you to the hospital, get you patched up, then I'll call your Laura May, tell her what happened."

Sure, just put Vern Withers back together again. Nothing to it, right? What had happened to leave the poor bastard in such horrible shape? Vern must be in worse shock than she was, way he was grinning like that.

And smoking. No, not a cigarette. His clothing. Or maybe it was his flesh she smelled, what was left of it.

Ellen turned away, picked up her radio mike, tried not to inhale the stench. Fortunately, she had too much to do to have to keep eyeballing the sizzling cop. She didn't think her stomach could stand much more.

She was seeing spots at the corners of her vision. Bad sign. She bit her lip hard so she didn't pass out. Her mind raced to stay ahead of the panic attack nipping away at her thoughts. Just get the job done, get an ambulance, get backup, get Luckinbill, get it done, get it, get it, get it.

A hand—a very hot hand—dropped heavily to her shoulder. She winced, inched away from the injured officer's grasp, but his tightening grip moved with her.

Chapter Twenty-Six

What now? he thought.

Would he very shortly start to rise from his body and float heavenward? What about the tunnel and the living, loving light beyond? The indescribably beautiful music and the life review? Now that might be interesting.

Who'd greet him on the other side? Both parents, both brothers and his only sister survived him. Three out of four hardy grandparents remained, and the only evidence of the fourth was a grainy black-and-white photograph of a somber old man he couldn't recall ever meeting, although he'd heard about being bounced on the old man's bony knee on an occasion or two when he was quite young. He couldn't see a heavenly homecoming based on such a dubious connection bringing tears of joy to either soul.

He vaguely remembered a cousin who'd bought the farm in a car-train wreck on account of a liquor problem, but he wasn't sure drunks qualified for leading the sort of celestial, harp-music-in-the-background reception he was anticipating, not that he was trying to be in any way judgmental.

Or maybe this whole train of thought was worthless. Could be that when the blackness sets in there's nothing to replace it. Just more blackness and silence and sleep, forever and ever.

Or—nowhere was a horrible thought—you went to that other place for merely ruminating upon such atheistic theories, as the fundamentalists seemed to believe. If faith really did provide the only working key to eternal survival, he sure as hell looked locked out of a worthwhile future.

And of course he found that like with any thought, the more he thought about not thinking atheistic thoughts, the more he thought them. Dying was a bitch.

Steve Addams blinked.

Blinked?

He shifted focus. Bit the inside of his mouth. Ran his tongue over his teeth. Wriggled his brows. Scrunched up his nose.

What were the rules on dying? Shouldn't he be comatose or something? At least incoherent. Should he be able to make facial twitches even as his soul warmed up for its final journey? All the things they don't teach you...

He sniffed the air. The ground, really, as he couldn't move anything but face parts, and dirt was the nearest substance to his nostrils. He was lying flat, of that he was reasonably certain, but can the dying pursue logical thought? *I think, therefore I'm not.*

He smelled soil and night and something like iron. His still-attuned mind knew the source of that smell: blood.

His.

He remembered the nightmare creatures and his old partner Vern, the bastard. All too clearly recalled his own ripped jugular and the way his breath and blood had gurgled out of the jagged hole. Even now as he puzzled over his confounded fate, he could feel the last black-red ounces pumping from him like an almost-played-out oil well.

But still he could breathe, and that proved something, didn't it? He inhaled deeply, felt his lungs fill with yellow moonlight.

He hadn't noticed that before, the way that the odd light all about him had a shape, a substance. He could feel it now, tickling his insides, filling up his pain-wracked body with soothing essence.

Pain? No, not really, come to think of it. Not anymore. A long, long time ago, a minute or an hour or a day ago, he'd lain there paralyzed in a sea of agony, just waiting to die, but that was before the misty moonlight like none he'd ever seen before had numbed him, had filled him with miraculous energy, an explosion of renewal.

He heard a sound. A good sign, his unimpaired hearing, because that was the sense that had been most affected by his predicament. He'd felt the world go cottony, and the fade-out had made sense at first as his mind filled with the inevitability of death. Nothing mattered. All hope had seeped away like his lifeblood.

But now, with hope suddenly returning aboard that miraculous yellow moonlight, now the presence of sound was a new and wonderful and life-affirming thing.

He listened.

The sound came from below. His body shifted ever so slightly— movement was still difficult—so that he could be sure of the source.

The ground, definitely.

The soil was red where Vern had ripped him up and tossed him out. A red muck, with another color added; a color he couldn't begin to describe, where a tangible mist of that moonlight had mingled with soil and his spilled life source.

It was here, on that quiet street beneath this blood-rich soil, that the sound, a tearing, uprooting noise, came. Something was shifting aside dirt and grass, worming its way to the top.

Steve Addams blinked, waited and saw. First, soil pushed out like sawdust before the drill bit, and then the plant poked through.

Not too unusual, the plant, except for its impressive rate of growth. Green, of course, as any healthy young plant should be. Dark green, almost black. Spiky, and perhaps its many limbs grew unusually dense, but not so amazing until he saw that the end of each limb gleamed like mirror shards, like metallic thorns, like polished shish-kebob stakes.

The plant turned, bent toward the injured man as if Steve Addams were the sun.

He smiled. This was right and proper, whatever was happening, whatever was going to happen. He felt it like he felt the light of the yellow moon.

The prongs purpled, reached for him. The plant owned countless fingers, each fingernail of sharpest steel.

It caressed the man on the ground. Stretched, teased, coyly encircled the young officer's head so pale, so bloodless.

One thing Steve Addams knew: it wouldn't hurt. The yellow moonlight he breathed so deeply assured him of this. He inhaled the promise, the promise of eternal life, with every expansion of his powerful lungs. He was cold with sweat, warm with hope.

Tenderly, the plant reached into his ears, his mouth, his eyes, his nose, and explored.

Steve Addams found Truth. He found that the yellow moon lies.

He screamed. Oh, how he screamed.

Chapter Twenty-Seven

Thad and Megan Crocker were probably the only sane people left in the police station when all of the electrically controlled cell doors clicked open and Vern Withers made his grand entrance.

While dozing in the officers' break room, they'd heard Ellen's brittle voice and Tom Luckinbill's edgy reply some time ago. Then the front door had slammed shut and the prisoners—only momentarily silenced by the brief, sharp interruption—resumed their mindless murmurings.

Megan had taken her husband's hand without knowing whether she was comforting him or she needed the contact to preserve her own delicate grasp on sanity. It probably worked both ways.

"I'll bet Tom heard something," Thad had said. "Something good. News."

"We could ask Ellen." She spoke through clenched teeth to keep the terror from escaping the pit of her stomach.

Thad nodded. "We could."

But they hadn't moved. They stayed on the sea-green vinyl couch in the break room where they'd spent most of the past couple hours. They could have waited across the street at the town hall with most of the other parents, but felt they'd get the freshest news in the police station. Although their clammy skin clung and squeaked with tension-induced sweat against plastic, the couch was still the most comfortable piece of furniture available. The downside was that the small room, consisting of not much more than the couch, a couple vending machines and a coffee-maker, was at the end of a corridor lined with jail cells. In a town the size and reputation of Cleary, Ohio, the most dangerous prisoner on any shift was likely to be a sleeping drunk, so no one minded eating lunch this close to the incarcerated.

Normally that was the case, as if the Crockers even remembered normal times.

At several minutes past midnight they heard the metallic click.

Thad twitched next to her. "What was that?"

Megan hated to say what she suspected. She'd heard the sound several times that day. There were two ways to open the cell doors: manually, with a set of keys, or electronically from a switch located near the dispatcher. Only, who would be releasing those doors with no one in the cell corridor and virtually the entire police force out on the streets?

"Thad..." she said.

The door opened that separated lobby from cell area. She vaguely recognized the profile of the officer darkly outlined at the other end of the long corridor.

Her husband moved into the break room doorway to get a better-lit view. "Vern?" He sounded cautious, doubtful.

She pulled him back into the room. She didn't know why, and presumably neither did Thad, but he went willingly.

She could vaguely detect a faint smile playing on Vern Withers's lips, or maybe it was just the unnatural way his mouth was pulled.

"I'll be right with you folks," the cop said. His voice was garbled. It sounded as ruined as his face.

He moved a few steps closer, and Megan could see a white bone sticking up behind one ear. His lower lip drooled uselessly. One arm was scraped to the bone. His uniform had been torn from his body in places. In others, it seemed to have been charred onto him, which would account for the horrible smell.

Her stomach twisted as Megan began to realize that Ellen Cooney probably wouldn't answer if called.

Vern Withers's legs didn't seem to be working well. He half-dragged himself to a cell door and opened it. He motioned for the strangers to claim their new freedom, and they did. He opened two more doors and filled the narrow hall with shuffling, mumbling humanity.

Albert Durwood stood free like the others. The killer carefully studied Megan and Thad as he stretched stiff muscles. Scratched his crotch. Licked his lips. Said, "Do you two really think I didn't see you?" His voice was hollow, lost. "I know the entire Crocker family. Love to tell you what Ben's been up to, but don't have the time."

Durwood caught Vern's attention with a snap of his fingers, and the cop responded with a nod. The killer turned again to the Crockers and said, "Got things to do. Got to start a brand-new society. But Vern can stick around awhile."

A grandmotherly voice rose from the demented crowd to sing out, "Dears, if you see my Tina, be sure to tell her Melba can take care of herself. Always could, don't matter what she thought."

Albert Durwood laughed at the old woman's misguided pleasantries, then fell into the night with the others.

All of the others except Vern Withers.

Megan watched, fascinated with fear, as the ruined police officer dragged himself slowly forward. His body looked to be relearning the fine art of walking, but learning fast.

"Vern, what is this?"

Thad's voice sounded more stable than he must have felt. He moved a few steps to stand between her and the advancing cop. "Vern, I'm talking to you."

A rusty chuckle somehow escaped the law officer's ruined throat. Then he bull-charged the last several feet of corridor and tackled Thad. The two crashed to the floor.

Megan jumped aside, her eyes flitting for a weapon. There were guns somewhere, had to be all kinds of them—it was a police station, for chrissake—but she had no idea where to begin looking. No time to search.

Vern snarled like a wild beast. Thad cried out.

As her eyes locked on the thing rolling on the floor with her husband, the thing that used to be a policeman, she knew Thad would be dead in about thirty seconds. The policeman-creature was changing even as it straddled him. As it raised its fist, she watched the back of its head crack like a hard-boiled egg peeling its shell. From beneath, a new head peeked through. Something black and small.

The police officer's shirt seam split and more leathery blackness poked through.

Bubbly sounds from Thad.

Megan made a fist and smashed through the snack machine against the far wall. Ignoring the pain and the specks of blood she dribbled onto the potato chip packages, she pulled free a shard of glass and stepped forward.

The Withers-thing had both hands—claws, really, she could see by looking over its shoulder—wrapped around her husband's neck. Thad's face was changing to a dangerously cool shade of blue.

Megan raised her glass shard and plunged it into the back of the creature's head. It snarled, turned to face her, loosening its grip on her husband.

The shard snapped in half. It wasn't glass at all, but plastic. There was more blood on her own hand where she'd gripped the substandard weapon than there was on the creature's skull. It raised one hand and swatted her across the room.

Megan crashed into the snack machine and sprawled to the floor. She felt like she'd dived into icy water, water so cold that it staggers your system so you can't tell hot from cold, pain from pleasure. All she immediately felt was a sharp and definite sense of nerve contact.

She shook her head. Watched the monster pound at her husband with the hand that had distractedly swatted her. Thad's legs jerked spasmodically.

"Son of a bitch," she screamed. She crawled over to the snack machine, again reached in, flung aside chips, crackers, pretzels, breath mints, and candy bars until her hand found one of the metal rods supporting the dangling snacks. She grabbed it, tore it from its mounting.

It hurt like hell to stand, but she managed to limp the three or four steps it took to reach what, in the hazy past, had been Vern Withers.

Megan used to be on nodding terms with Vern's wife, Laura May. Round, nervous woman with colorless hair and a hesitant smile. She'd see Laura May at the town hall sometimes during council meetings. Megan could never have guessed she'd attempt murder on the other woman's spouse to keep him from inflicting the same upon her own husband. It would have been the height of bad taste to even imagine such offensiveness.

The flat fact of the matter—the kill-or-be-widowed aspect of the whole situation—was the final impetus she needed. Megan raised the metal rod and brought it down, nearly taking off the creature's scalp. The beastly snarl turned high-pitched as its head flopped to an unnatural angle.

Like double vision, she saw a new head rising from the bloodied decay of the old. This one was nearly round with deep-set eyes and a wide mouth and no other features. It was like a clay depiction of humanity, a hurried model dashed together by someone with little artistic talent. She was confused, couldn't remember which head she'd attacked.

Had to concentrate. Megan again raised the metal rod, and this time buried it into the creature's new temple, the softest place to enter the brain if the thing that had once been Vern Withers even had one.

The rod nearly disappeared into the forming flesh. It was more than soft, her point of entry; it was unfinished, like the cushiony back of a baby's head.

Brain matter and pus accumulated at the wound.

The creature tilted, slipped off her husband like a building crumbling to the implosive effects of dynamite.

She was too late. She knew, just knew, that the Withers-creature had won. Her husband wasn't moving. She crouched over him, stepping into the sticky fluid spilling from two bodies. Thad's hand felt limp and cool in hers.

Her strength was gone. She started to cry.

He squeezed her hand. Now she could hear his rasping breath. Thad coughed, choked.

She gasped. Kissed him, letting her tears wash the blue of oxygen deprivation from his face. "I don't ever want to lose you," she whispered.

Chapter Twenty-Eight

He'd had nightmares make more sense than this long evening, Tom thought as he braked in front of Jeff Smith's demolished cruiser in the middle of Irv Coy's soybean field near Route 35.

He turned off the ignition, rolled down the window and listened to his ticking engine and the crickets in the trees bordering the field. Fireflies winked like exploding suns in distant galaxies. A solitary moth perched and preened on a wiper blade. With all that had been going on around him, Tom found such serenity just beyond the town limits hard to comprehend.

He was at the site of the second police wreck that hour. Baylog and Fleming were helping scrape the county deputies Kempton and Wade from the accident on Bridge Street. From the bits and pieces of witness statements he'd been able to pick up listening in on calls to Ellen, it looked like they'd been hit—deliberately, it had seemed to some observers—by a local cop car, hit-and-run style. Vern Withers had simply walked away, as if in a daze, from his ruined ride.

And what was Withers doing without Addams, anyway? Ellen had received a priority call from Steve just minutes before the head-on. Was Steve still in the car Vern abandoned? Was the body count mounting faster than Tom could keep track?

Tom had been on his way to check the Crocker place as a result of that confusing call when he'd intercepted the latest news flash: Jeff in some kind of trouble off the road somewhere by the highway. With a thundering heart, he altered his course to take a look. After all, if the boys were at the Crockers', they must be safe.

It hadn't taken long to pick up the other cruiser's tire tracks in the mushy soil. He'd followed a clear trail of uprooted soybeans straight to the wreck.

There was no way Tom could have recognized the other vehicle without a hint of what to expect. He had only twisted metal and splintered glass to go by.

"Oh, Jeff," he pleaded. He'd always wanted his own boys to grow up to be like Jeff Smith. Felt that if he could entrust them to the young cop, something might rub off, a sort of character osmosis that would fill them with openness and trust, quiet decency; temper the hard frame of inflexibility they'd inherited from their old man.

He could hear nothing, saw no movement in the wreckage. How'd Jeff gotten out here in the middle of nowhere? And why?

The questions kept piling up. Like, why had he heard no response to Jeff's emergency call from Ellen? And his boys...his boys...?

Tom used all of his professional discipline to examine the evening's only piece of good news. Apparently, Steve Addams had spotted the missing kids, and they were heading toward the Crocker place. That's exactly where Tom would be if he hadn't intercepted this call.

There always seemed to be something—or someone—keeping him from them. A job, a mother, a series of bizarre catastrophes. But not after tonight, that was for sure. He stepped hesitantly out of the car. He'd tried radioing for an ambulance as soon as he'd spotted the wreck, but hadn't been too surprised at being unable to raise Ellen or anyone else. The world as he knew it was ending, so nothing more could shock him.

Tom stiffly made his way to the dead car, in no hurry to confront what he knew he'd find. The air smelled rusty with roasted metal, but there was no fire. Despite the silence, he could almost hear the screams that must have broken the night not long before.

The moonlight seemed strange as it glittered off a billion shards of broken glass. It was a shade of yellow that irrationally increased his fears.

His foot kicked aside mechanical parts and sheet metal he no longer recognized. He found a shoulder harness still locked in place but cut apart as if the wearer had been pulled violently from it.

He didn't need this, didn't need to see...

When he found the body some thirty feet from the wreckage, Tom's stomach heaved, but he managed to keep down lunch, whenever and whatever that had been.

It was Kerri. He could tell by the relatively unburnt legs, smooth and thinner than Jeff's. Not much thinner, he thought with a wry chuckle that didn't belong to the scene.

She had no head.

Tom stepped back, almost tripping over the evening's second headless surprise.

He groaned, doubled over and, like a kid at his first keg party, puked on his shoes.

He felt better; not much, but some. "Jeff, what happened here?" he asked the charred remains, as if he expected an answer.

He got one.

"It's not so bad, Tom. You ought to try it."

He stared at the headless corpse, figuring that he now knew how mental collapse felt.

"Not there," the voice said. "Here."

Tom had seen without really seeing the bush by the wreckage. Now he watched as the sharp leaves parted and a small head stared him down. Jeff's head, but three-quarters the original size.

Jeff-the-head smiled brightly. "Come on, big guy. Just give yourself over. It's gonna happen anyway, since Durwood and the Crocker kid let the other side in. It's really pretty interesting."

Tom fell. His legs simply gave out, and one cheek hugged the cool ground. He smelled vegetation that must have been soybeans, although he had no idea what soybeans were supposed to smell like. He closed his eyes and waited for the nightmare to end. Maybe when he awoke—

"Come on, Luckinbill. Get up, you're embarrassing yourself," a second voice piped in. "You want to see Greg and Tony again, don't you?"

Tom rose to a sitting position. "Greg and Tony?"

Two more bush limbs parted to frame the impaled head of Kerri Upshaw.

"That's right," the Kerri-head said. "They're on their way to see Ben Crocker right now."

"And they're real anxious to run into you," Jeff-the-head added mischievously.

Tom shook his head. Didn't know what he was denying, only that he couldn't let himself accept.

"You think *you're* surprised," the Jeff-head said with another chuckle. "You should have seen us. Right, Kerri?"

"It gets better," the woman's head replied. "This is just the first step. It's amazing what we've picked up already. You know, just hanging around."

"No, no, no," Tom said. Quietly. Firmly. The sensible tone he'd used to get the boys to eat meals from their highchairs.

"Oh, yes," Jeff-the-head said. "See for yourself." He knew he should look away, should close his eyes, should run screaming from this hellish soybean field in the hideous moonlight. But he saw. Tom Luckinbill's glance fell into the deep, black pools of his young officer's eyes.

And he saw...

"We've got to go back," Greg says. "He's my brother, and he's lost."

Ben Crocker shakes his head so hard that Tom, the secret voyeur from nowhere, hears teeth rattling. "We can't. I'm not going, and neither's Danny. If you take off, we leave you behind."

Greg says, "Tony wouldn't abandon you, Crocker. How can you not help him? He's probably in trouble."

"He knew the risks," young Ben spits back. "Isn't that right, Trevor? Danny?"

The other two nod grimly.

Greg takes a deep breath. "All right," he says, starting to walk away alone. "I'll find him myself."

The night glows with yellow moonlight of an even deeper and more alien shade than the one under which Tom is now standing or hopes he's still standing. Reality has taken several gymnastic flips.

The terrain of this alien landscape surrounding his boys is woodsy, unfamiliar

Don't go, Greg, Tom mind shouts. Too late. He gone. The boy can't hear his father, who can only listen and watch: a parent's ultimate hell.

Greg is swallowed by the black forest under the alien moon.

The other three boys cut the still air with crude laughter. "Let him go," Ben says.

"Good riddance," adds Danny Young, with a giggle.

"His own fault "Ben says. "We tried to tell him."

He was falling for miles and miles...

Tom braced himself with two hands on the cool ground, stopping the dizzying sensation. A stab of pain so intense that Tom didn't at first even know its location—it was everywhere—brought him fully back. That and quiet laughter, the sound made by what remained of Jeff Smith.

"Hey, boss, you'll get into it. Honest. Look at all the long conversations we can have, just the three of us."

Tom gasped as the plant tendril burrowed deeper into his pant leg just below one knee. His whole body spasmed in violent reaction.

"It only hurts at first," Jeff-head said gently.

Tom Luckinbill screamed.

"Don't be such a baby about it," the Kerri-thing scolded.

The bush limb slithering into Tom's skin began just under the Jeff-head, a half-dozen feet away.

"You don't have a choice in the matter," the Jeff-head said, lifting an eyebrow. "Just let things work out."

The pain was fire. Tom grabbed his service revolver, his palm so sweaty he could barely maintain a grip. He heard the plant breaking more skin, then begin to pull him toward the bush, closer to Jeff Smith's severed head.

He was a fish on a hook, and something was reeling him in.

He'd never fired at someone before. Now he aimed it at what passed for his favorite cop.

Tom's fiery leg was preceding him to his certain and horrible death. He snapped up soybean roots and etched five-fingered gullies in the soft soil in a futile effort to keep his distance. His upraised leg was now about all that separated him from Jeff in the accursed bush.

Tom aimed at the Jeff-head but found his own foot in the way. Exerting all of the remaining strength he had, he tugged at the plant limb, pulled his foot back just far enough to remove it from the line of fire.

The Jeff-head lost its smile. "You wouldn't," he said.

He couldn't. Tom couldn't shoot Jeff, couldn't shoot another human being virtually point-blank. Couldn't—

His gun roared. The crickets ceased their excited chatter. The Jeff-head screamed as it exploded into Jackson Pollock splatters of a liquid substance closer in color and consistency to sap than to blood.

"Now you've done it," the Kerri-thing snarled, lapping away at skull-matter painting her cheeks.

Tom scooted away from the bush, grimacing as he yanked out the limp tendril from his leg. It tickled a muscle as it reversed direction from his open wound. Most of the searing pain dissolved, leaving him almost ashamed of his agonized outburst of moments before.

The Kerri-head cackled. "Too late. You'll find out for yourself. Hey Tom, take a look at these hot new pierced earrings of mine."

She was referring to the plant branches twining into and out of her skull. With a crackle, the bush began to reclaim Kerri-the-head into its mysterious folds. Before completely disappearing, she shouted, "Jeff's on your conscience too, along with the boys. Remember that, Tom— and you will."

Yes, Greg and Tony, he thought as he rose shakily to his feet. His trousers were ripped, and a few bright blood speckles further ruined his uniform blues, but his leg was no worse off than sore. Wouldn't slow him down a bit. He'd find Greg and Tony and everything would be all right. Their mother couldn't possibly stay mad if Tom found their boys before she got there. She'd let him see them whenever he wanted, and that would be frequently.

That would be nice. Find Greg and Tony and get that unfaithful ex-wife off his case and everything would work out fine.

Find Greg and Tony.

Yes. Find.

Chapter Twenty-Nine

Talk about your up-and-down days. Bad as his had begun, who'd have imagined it could turn out this spectacularly? The woman with the legs up to here moaned deeply while she straddled Carl Thayer, shimmied upward, arched, twisted her hipbone, raised her short skirt, and guided his face toward heaven...

A bit earlier in the evening, Carl had muttered something to Bob Carmichael while signaling Donny behind the bar for a refill. What was it, his fourth? His brows closed in even tighter over his drooping eyelids in a futile effort to pull two answers out of his fuzzled brain at once: How many bourbons and Coke? And what had he been muttering to Bob Carmichael about? He'd forgotten, already.

"Don't matter what you think, Carl," the other man said, stabbing a finger and a cigarette at his friend's chest. "You go paranoid like this, Carl, you wind up like them out there. In jail or a psycho ward or scrounging from a garbage can. Then other people can talk about you same way we talk about them out there."

Now he remembered. Carl Thayer's jaw dropped in disbelief at how misled some people could be. "So I'm lying, then."

"Didn't say that at all, Carl. I think it's more a matter of—"

"Imagining things? Look out the window, Bob Carmichael. Go ahead. You see something you never seen before. Not in Cleary, you haven't. You see armies of them. Armies of the night." Carl liked that, liked it a lot: *Armies of the night.* It had a certain ring to it, it certainly did.

"Don't see nothing at all out there," Bob Carmichael replied. "Too dark, and that...I don't know, but the light's kinda playing tricks."

"Fruitcake armies," the broad in the mini said, the one with the legs. She sputtered coy laughter at the audacity of her interruption.

"Whatever," Carl grumbled, never comfortable arguing with women. Or even talking to them, least not ones like the one who'd planted herself on the bar stool next to him, just walking in all alone like she belonged there at Little Al's with Carl and Bob Carmichael, and Donny behind the bar.

"Sure," Bob Carmichael said. "There's something wrong here. Wouldn't doubt it for a minute, though I wouldn't get so dramatic as calling them folks an army. Anyway, Tom Luckinbill's taking care of things."

"Tom Luckinbill." Carl snorted.

"What's that mean?" Donny Parks wanted to know. He was positioned as usual when not serving: braced on both elbows behind the bar, gazing rapturously at whatever silent picture was playing on the TV mounted in the corner. At that particular moment, he seemed to be lip-reading a *Cheers* rerun. Donny watched his silent comedies with the same respectful, humorless concentration he gave sports or equally silent soaps or game shows or his friends Phil, Sally Jessy and Oprah.

Now Donny was staring at Carl with a damned-near interested expression on his pale face. "You got a problem with Tom Luckinbill?" he asked gently, curiously.

"Wouldn't if he followed through more," Carl answered, speaking right up. "I tried warning him early today when I caught the first of these nutcakes. He had a good ole time of it, though, that's all. He and the Smith kid had all kinds of chuckles over what the asshole did to the side of my gas station, and now this town is overrun with their kind. Whose fault might that be, Donny? You decide."

"Hmm," the bartender replied, managing to sound neither interested nor bored, agreeable nor disagreeable. He turned back to the tube, maybe trying to figure which environment, his or Sam Malone's, more closely resembled barroom reality.

"Well, it's that other thing," Bob Carmichael said.

"What other thing?"

Carl's best buddy finished his Bud with a gulp and brightly suggested to Donny the possibility that he might consume another, as if this were a unique idea.

Carl, with a half inch of fluid remaining in his glass, mostly ice runoff, thought of matching Bob's purchase with one of his own, but decided against it. Carl Thayer was a loud, rambunctious man who smoked too much, gambled, insulted friends, and bullied service station customers, but there were two things he didn't do: drink too much (usually) or fool around (ever).

"I'm talking about," Bob Carmichael began, "that other stuff you said. About how this guy, the stranger, the bum, how he messed with your mind. That's the part I'm finding hard to deal with."

Carl Thayer's first instinct was to jump down his best friend's throat and come out with the voice box that had questioned his credibility. Instead he mumbled, "Gimme a cigarette," waited for the demand to be met, then took his time lighting and sucking and puffing.

"You seem honest enough to me," the redhead with the leather miniskirt and torso-hugging blouse chirped in for no apparent reason. Who'd said anything to her? And, for chrissake, what was she doing on this side of Cleary Center when Ray's Place was on the opposite end? She get lost or something? Most nights it was just Carl and Bob Carmichael and Donny and one or two other men at Little Al's, and that suited him just fine.

Carl carefully sorted through his various late-night thoughts:

—He was starting on his fifth bourbon and Coke, a personal best.

—The beer commercial now on the tube looked more interesting than the show.

—Say what you wanted about Little Al's, how it looked downright depressing next to The Bluegrass or Ray's, where the kids hung out. Linoleum floor and vinyl bar stools, but it had the sharpest little Jap TV he'd ever laid eyes on. Could almost walk right through the picture tube and ask Woody for a cool one soon as he was done refilling Norm.

—So dark outside. And weird. Like the four of them were the only ones left anywhere.

While one part of his mind ran down all these bits and pieces of thoughts, the hardest-working part was chewing himself out for talking too much about the wild scene in front of his garage earlier in the day. Old Bob Carmichael was as gullible as God made them, but even he had questioned Carl's reaction to the stranger. Good thing Carl hadn't gone into any details, mentioned the way the eye from nowhere glared down at him, peeked into the most private regions of his mind. And how that tunnel had opened up in front of him, and that *thing* had come out and gone right for him, crawled right down his throat like that.

Carl shuddered. "Eat shit, Bob old buddy," he said. "I'm out of here. Donny, come take my money."

"Watch out for those vicious hobos, Carl," his friend cackled.

"Me too, if you don't mind," the woman in the leather skirt said.

Carl and Bob Carmichael exchanged puzzled, almost worried glances. It was several seconds before her meaning became even halfway apparent.

"You, uh, you need a ride?" Carl hoped she didn't.

"Thanks," she said. "I mean, if it's no bother."

He saw Bob Carmichael arch an eyebrow, lower his head and snicker, bringing both middle-aged men right back to their school days.

Carl cleared his throat. "No, I guess...no. It's okay. Not out of the way." Now how'd he know what "out of the way" was when he had no idea where the damn girl lived?

Donny scooped up his money, pecked silently at the new cash register. It was a computer, like everything else. Just what the bar needed: a nearly silent cash drawer, as if reducing the noise level at Little Al's was a worthwhile goal. Donny slapped a few coins down on the bar, then resumed his position underneath the Jap TV, but his glance kept sneaking back to Carl and his new and well-built friend.

No, she didn't belong in Ray's, where the college kids hung out in jeans and baggies without socks. Maybe with the dance crowd at the

Glass Frog. Her outfit was too dangerous for The Bluegrass and just plain a waste of good skin for Little Al's. Al's was a place to sit and drink and watch sports and grumble about your take-home pay and how little you get to take back out once you get home. It was for a man whose only reaction to a leather miniskirt was to hope it wasn't exposing his own daughter. Little Al's was home away from home for the man who knew that women were taking over the world; for the man who needed shelter from the storm. For the man whose woman was killing him with attention, not for one looking for extracurricular female contact.

All right, that's not *all* that came to Carl Thayer's mind when he saw the young woman with legs up to here. A part of him stirred, the part that hadn't been stirring much as of late, truth be known. But he sincerely believed that all fifty-something men of working-class means fell into two categories when it came to young things with miniskirts and legs: those wanting and not getting, and those taking up more realistic hobbies like bourbon and television.

Or at least that was the way he thought—if he'd ever thought to think such thoughts—until the redhead with the legs asked him to take her home.

"Here, let me get the door."

That line, in a gruff, nonchalant tone of voice, was more for the benefit of Bob Carmichael and Donny, like he could convince them that this sort of thing happened every time he wandered into a watering hole, forget the fact that Bob Carmichael and Donny knew better if anyone did.

Once outside, Carl's Roger Moorish veneer began to crack in the strange light.

"Interesting evening," the woman said, looking up into the sky.

"Yeah." Seemed that was all he could force out of his dry throat. What was he doing? He'd never cheated before; not on account of his great love for Peggy or because he felt bound and gagged by moral constraints, but because he recognized himself as being in the great majority of men who will spend their entire lives looking attractive to, at best, one woman. And probably even those days were behind him.

Anyway, that downright scary moonlight all around him was affecting his train of thought, keeping him from concentrating on pickup lines or much of anything else.

"My car," he said. "I think it's over here." He squinted, found it easily in the nearly deserted gravel lot. The Plymouth sat next to Carmichael's Chevy truck. He couldn't help smirking at the thought of how his buddy was going to be driving home alone, unlike Carl here.

"Unh," he said, a hand wave indicating ownership of the Plymouth. He clawed through his mind for guidance: Should he hold her door, or would that too closely resemble a date or look sexist to the bimbo? Or was he going to lose points if he didn't extend the old-fashioned courtesy?

The mere thought of dating brought him back to reality. All he was doing was providing free taxi service. He'd deposit her home with barely a mumbled goodbye and probably not even get a peck on the cheek for his efforts.

He heard a siren in the distance, and for one panicky moment figured it was the law closing in. But it was only an ambulance, he was pretty sure. Anyway, what did he have to feel guilty for? Yet.

"I really do appreciate this," she said. "The ride."

"Yeah, the ride. No problem." He turned the ignition over and his wipers dragged whiningly over a dry windshield. "Sorry," he said, then felt like a dolt both because it looked like he couldn't operate simple machinery and because he'd followed up the minor gaffe of accidentally flicking his wiper switch with an apology that only drew more attention to it.

He pulled out of the lot and asked, "Which way?"

She shrugged. Giggled. "I don't know. Which way do you prefer?"

That's when Carl Thayer started to sweat.

He kept rerunning each very recent scene on the black screen of his mind while the movie that had become his life got wilder and wilder. So unbelievable, so utterly unfathomable, he felt that if he didn't immediately commit what was happening to memory, he'd lose the vaporous reality for all time.

If only Bob Carmichael could see him now.

Well, not *right* now, Carl amended. Right now he had a five-eight redhead with the kind of leg tone that ripples with every pavement-slapping step; had her wrapped across his lap, her leather skirt hiked up and thighs hot and pliable enough to prove that the lady didn't prefer Hane's or any sort of feminine foundation.

He only knew all this by sense of feel, on account of the way her chest kept interrupting his gaze. Not her white blouse, though; that had been unbuttoned and shoved aside; maybe by her, maybe by him, it was so hard to remember with his alcohol intake and that confusing moonlight and all.

She was breathing more harshly now, sometimes moaning a bit, as she rubbed her cool breasts against his grizzled face. He sucked appreciatively on first one hard little nipple, then the other. His mouth was wet with his-and-hers saliva, his lips sore from hard kisses.

Oh, God, if this wasn't heaven...

He shifted, and she recontorted to fit her tanned hard-body once more against his. Her indelicate squirming motion made him groan with pain and pleasure. Jesus, the meat between his legs had to be ten inches long by now and weigh as much as a leg. He hadn't felt that fully utilized since puberty.

She lifted her body slightly—a difficult movement due to the Plymouth's restrictive backseat—and moved a hand under her own ass, leveraging it off of his lap. The movement slipped one warm tit out of Carl's mouth long enough for a quick peek out the side window.

He thought he'd heard something. Had been thinking along those lines ever since turning off the engine. He'd flinched every time it ticked while cooling down, but their exposed positions hadn't seemed to affect the girl any.

Jesus, he didn't even know her name yet. Maybe he'd never learn it, it would just be like one of those anonymous *Penthouse Forum* letters he never quite believed.

Of course, he couldn't have seen a cop if the entire force was out there taking notes, directing traffic, and filming the act for posterity and Peggy's divorce lawyer. There was just too much hot breath steaming up the glass, and the moonlight was throwing indescribable shadows out there to the extent that he wasn't exactly sure what he was seeing. The world seemed tinted as if with that sickly shade of yellow that comes with tornado weather, though that wasn't exactly right, either. The light was...different.

Oh, well, it was probably just as well that he couldn't see whatever or whoever might be lurking out there. They were parked in the junior high lot, for chrissake. Could be they tack on an extra five years when they catch a middle-aged married man in a school parking lot with a redhead who's twenty-five, if that. Something like the automatic time they add to felonies committed with a gun. Well, he *was* using a gun of sorts, he thought giddily. A magnum, largest hand-held bastard in the universe.

And holding it was exactly what she was doing right now. Carl groaned, the way he thought only women did and only in those videotapes he sometimes rented when Peggy was visiting her mother. His eyes closed tightly in response to her hot-yet-cool touch.

Again she squirmed, corkscrewed herself right onto him, worked her way up his body like a stripper on a brass pole.

"Do me," she whispered.

Carl thought about it. He didn't even know where his arms were, scrunched up somewhere between the two bodies and probably fast asleep. And he wasn't quite sure what her request meant. It wasn't that he knew nothing about sex, just that he'd had so little recent practice, and nothing this experimental. Hadn't "done" his wife in about a quarter-century or so. Might be like getting on a bicycle, but just because you used to be able to ride a Schwinn doesn't mean you can handle a European racer.

Still she climbed his tensed form until her meaning became crystal clear. Carl closed his eyes once more, pursed his sore lips, and opened up.

He wasn't sure if he was doing things right, but the way the woman writhed told him he wasn't too far off base.

His mystery woman. There was something exotic, luxuriously decadent about backseating with a stranger. He was living a fantasy he'd never even fantasized, because such thoughts are a waste of time for middle-aged men who own small-town service stations and have been happily, or at least not unhappily married for twenty-nine years. Sean Connery gets this lucky, maybe, but not—

Carl Thayer tensed up in mid-nibble. It had been a long time since he'd engaged in anything remotely resembling such activity, true, but not so long that he'd forgotten basic female anatomy. While he couldn't begin to identify everything down there, he quite definitely knew what didn't belong on the tip of his tongue just then.

He gagged. Drew his head back as far as his neck would allow, shook it and somehow choked out the words, "No, no."

Despite his best efforts, Carl couldn't dislodge the disgusting object that was worming its way down his throat, moving rhythmically with the woman's every pelvic grind.

Nightmare time began as the hard thing grew to pornographic proportions, inched farther inside him, no doubt injecting him all at once with HIV, herpes, and homosexuality.

He couldn't breathe. His heart rammed his chest as if blaming him for the cut-off air supply. His eyes were open now, wide and unseeing. He somehow remembered his arms, pinned against his own body and tingly with interrupted blood flow. He pushed the leather skirt out of his line of vision, and feebly shoved aside her writhing groin.

At least now he could see her face. Could see her eyes, hard and emotionless. They were the eyes he'd seen before, in his vision when he'd touched the bum.

The skull split down the middle and something black and as leathery as the woman-thing's skirt emerged from the wreckage.

More sirens wailed in the too-far distance.

Carl Thayer shrieked, but the sound couldn't get past whatever it was—tasting also black and leathery—still inching its way down his throat.

Chapter Thirty

Beneath the music, Ben could hear the steady purr of a well-tuned engine somewhere behind him and gaining fast.

We'll trail and hunt you like game

We'll rape and torture and maim

We'll poke out an eye

And leave you to die

The words were pleasantly sung by a woman or man, a child or adult, by one or by several. Details didn't matter, just the lilting rhythm, soft and playful as a fairy tale accompanied by two or three simple instruments he couldn't quite identify. Ben wanted to hum along, to just pull his tired body over to the side of the street, lean against an old, sturdy tree, close his heavy eyelids and listen...listen...

Your body will stiffen and bloat

Your soul will leave you and float

He could now identify the comforting smells of gasoline and engine oil as the truck pulled closer still, but still unseen.

But nowhere near Heaven; oh, no

Just stop. His lungs hurt too much; he'd run too far, too fast...

To Hell you're bound, to Hell you'll go

Not yet, he wouldn't. Ben put on a burst of speed as his system suddenly pumped as much adrenaline as blood. Something tickled his arm: a moth. He cursed it, smashed it to dust and turned on more speed, more speed.

Making a split-second decision, he angled off of the street like a war-movie fighter pilot, breaking away from the squadron.

Out of the corner of an eye he caught a white patch of steady movement as the ice cream truck with its single scratchy speaker pulled up alongside.

Before seeing too much, he jumped the curb. He crossed a sidewalk, climbed a short hill, and found himself in the backyard of the Proctor Funeral Home.

It was a brightly lit, overly manicured lawn, the grass clipped short and as orderly as a well-planned death. Underfoot, it felt bristly, like turf.

Where the yard ended in back, a six-foot privacy fence began. It was made of birch or pine, and had brackets spaced every few feet for flowerpots. These he used like steps, crushing several bright plants, propelling himself up and over.

He landed in a heap in a much softer yard. Here the grass was tall, the ground rutted. The harsh yellow moonlight illuminated dark clumps of grass that stood even taller, tall enough to have been fertilized by dog shit.

Ben stopped, crouched. Now he had even more to worry about. His testicles crawled as he listened for the telltale rattle of chains and the deep-throated growl of a territorial pit bull. He heard only the faraway lilt of truck engine and music. He stretched, began to move again.

The street out front was Chamberlain. Ben's home was on Merryside, the next one over and three blocks down.

He stooped behind a severely sculpted bush near the sidewalk and peered out. No foot traffic, no cars. No dogs sniffing the cool night air for action, and only dark windows at the houses lining the street. He looked upon a world he no longer knew, contaminated with the twin unfamiliarities of yellow moonlight and the empty nocturnal outdoors.

He checked his wrist, then remembered leaving home that day—yesterday?—without his watch. Funny, but none of his friends had asked for the time; almost like it didn't matter out there in that other place where forever was a single minute and the minutes could last for centuries and the moon was eternal.

The ice cream truck would be waiting for him on Chamberlain. He felt reasonably safe behind the shrub, but knew that as soon as his feet found pavement, the truck would find him. He scrunched down, crossed his arms and plotted his next move.

He and Danny had split up on Becker Street once they'd thrown off whatever Trevor had become, and headed their separate ways to the perceived protection of home. "See ya tomorrow," Danny had shouted before gliding from sight. The boy's high voice had sounded damned near normal, like the entire day could be canceled with a casual goodbye. Listening to his surviving friend's fading footfalls, Ben had waited tensed for screams that never came.

Danny was safe, Ben convinced himself. But why had they split up like those sorry assholes in the sequeled-to-death slasher flicks?

Because they'd both tried convincing themselves that things were normal again, that was why. They'd separated where their routes home diverged, their tenacious young minds refuting the Trevor-thing and the stalking ice cream truck.

Ben heard a siren from afar, or from just down the street. Hard to tell anymore, sound being as hazy as the yellow atmosphere.

He made up his mind. Hunched low like a racer at the starting block waiting for the pistol crack, Ben shoved off with one foot, jacking his thin arms to and fro while gulping air into lungs already starting to flame out. His heart thundered with panic, but with exhilaration as well. There was nothing so liberating, so downright anarchistic as slapping deserted pavement in the black of night. He threw out all the mental baggage weighing him down, reduced himself to a strong, dependable young package of lungs and heart and muscle and fists.

Yes...!

Let them come, the bastards. Let them try to take him. He swatted a moth on a collision course with his face, and the ice cream music tinkling louder in the distance only pushed him harder, faster. He could have taken on Rickey Henderson, Neon Deion, anyone foolish enough to challenge him. He slashed across streets, cut through yards, trampled gardens, jumped fences. Canine teeth snapped and porch lights flared in his wake, but nothing stopped him as he accelerated through obstacles, past one familiar landmark after another.

For Skippy.

For Greg and Tony.

For Danny (good luck, pal).

And most of all for Trevor, the *real* Trevor Kincaid.

He had to survive simply because so many others hadn't. He'd make it, simple as that.

Most things, you see your mom about. But when the situation's really serious, and there's absolutely no way around it, you go to Dad. Ben Crocker doubled his odds by calling out for both parents as he hurtled up his front porch and flung himself through the unlocked screen door.

No one answered.

His heart pounded so loud he wasn't sure he'd hear even if they did respond. His stomach burned and a sound like the ocean roared in his head. He tore through every room, even into the dark basement, before admitting the truth.

There was no one home.

Back upstairs, Ben glanced at his folks' bedside clock. It was nearly 2:00 a.m. No one home? That reality—abandonment by his parents in the wee hours of his young life—was as unreal as the moonlight creeping in through the open windows to make hulking monsters out of familiar furniture.

"In here, Ben."

At last. He wheeled, searched the blocky shadows without finding the source of his father's voice.

"No. Here. In the bathroom."

Ben could see the hallway quite clearly, filled as it was with yellow moonlight. It seemed to glow, float, bathed in the unspeakable substance he'd brought back with him. He flicked light switches, every switch he found, accomplishing nothing more than adding artificial glow to the alien light source that teased his tired eyes to tears of frustration and fear.

He moved slowly to the bathroom, keeping his hands away from the light-washed walls as if the indefinite color could rub off, could infect him like it had infected Trevor and the others.

The bathroom was lavender. It had impossibly small finger towels folded delicately into wicker baskets. It smelled of disinfectant and lilac and soap and mysterious herbs of no known value.

"Come closer, Ben. Good. Now look down."

The Dad voice came from the sink drain.

"Good job, boy. You and Danny, you invited them in, son. You helped them big time when you opened the way for Trevor, and now they've got me."

His father's voice wheezed, choked, chuckled. "Just kidding, Ben. I'm not angry. Actually, your mom and I are having the time of our lives. It's hard to describe what it's like here, but you'll see for yourself soon enough. You get the credit, yessirree. None of this could have happened without you and your curious little friends.

"And speaking of friends, Ben...I'm sending you a little surprise. A token of our appreciation."

There was barely enough moisture in Ben's mouth to respond, but he managed to croak, "Surprise?" It was something to say, words to keep silence at bay.

"Well, two surprises, actually. It's good to have friends, don't you think, Ben?"

Something moved behind him, footsteps that had been muffled by the carpeted stairs. By the time Ben turned around, Greg and Tony stood behind him in the upstairs hallway.

The invisible father-voice laughed again, the sound ringing with metallic echo. "You boys go play now, you hear?"

The Luckinbill brothers' faces began to peel.

Chapter Thirty-One

The road flew past the high school, wound south of the interstate, and curved off toward the small town of Jasper Mills to the southeast. Megan turned to say something to her pale husband in the passenger seat of the Escort, but Thad didn't look well enough to care. He was hunched low, still breathing hard.

Now didn't seem to be the time to tell him that they were traveling a road that didn't exist, least hadn't until a couple minutes ago. That their otherwise dependable Ford had simply refused to deposit them in front of their home on Merryside where they could wait for Ben. Had instead opted for a midnight ride out to the country via a route Megan, a Cleary native, had never traveled. And that she couldn't do a thing about it except, like that Texas politician advised concerning another ignominy, sit back and enjoy it.

Or go insane. That seemed like a more realistic option about now. She felt her tires sinking even deeper into the springy surface. She gunned the engine in frustration. The Escort neither sped up nor slowed down, but kept to its steady fifty-six. From the now-distant center of town she could make out the blue and red flicker of dome lights and hear sirens wailing lonely and desperate.

Too little, too late.

Thad looked up. "I thought we were going to find Ben." His voice sounded incredibly strained and weak, almost gentle.

We're trying, Megan wanted to say. She opened her mouth with no real idea of what words were going to scramble out, but closed it again when she saw the crowd gathering in the field where the makeshift road ended.

Thad sat up straighter. In a raw rasp he said, "Don't like the look of this. Let's go around them."

At least he was making decisions again. Decisions that would have made a lot of sense if only she could comply. Her tires bit deeper into the corky pavement, as if emphatically nixing the suggestion.

Dead ahead, a lone figure stood apart from the crowd, arms raised. The Escort's headlights picked up the figure coming nearer, nearer, nearer as the car sped up. Megan ground her teeth and stiffened both legs against the expected impact.

Like a maestro finishing off an orchestra, the figure suddenly snapped his wrists and pumped his arms down to his body with the power of an Olympic breast stroker. The car slid to a sharp, shuddering halt with the front fender brushing the knees of the grinning Albert Durwood.

"Okay," Thad said. Just *okay*, nothing but weary acceptance in his voice now.

Megan felt as defeated as her husband sounded.

The human monster that was Albert Durwood rapped his knuckles sharply on the hood of their car, and beckoned them out like the perfect host. His arms were short, stout and pink, nearly hairless. His wide mouth could have swallowed the Escort. Shuffling strangers surrounded the vehicle like George-Romero-inspired nightmares.

Beyond the crowds she could see a barn, a distant cluster of trees marking the southernmost point of Waylock Park, and a faded billboard proclaiming Diane Seaton as the most logical candidate for Fayette County prosecutor. In the scraggly field, moths mingled by the thousands, the millions. Under the yellow light they looked like snow falling; dirty gray, erratic snow that was as likely to fall up as down. She knew this setting would permanently haunt her dreams, if ever she dreamt again.

Thad opened his car door.

"Get back in here," Megan ordered sharply. "Lock up and we'll—"

He broke her command with a patient head shake. "Won't do any good." He reached over and kissed her, wincing. His upper lip left a sweat trail on hers. "The road might forget about you if I keep Durwood busy. Whoever or whatever is controlling things, it wants this meeting to take place. Otherwise, we wouldn't be here. If you can, peel out and find Ben."

Then he was gone, leaving her to ponder his surreal message.

Most troubling of all, she had understood every word.

Chapter Thirty-Two

"Do you have any idea what you've put your mother and me through?"

The words were hissed rather than spoken. They started deep in the man's throat and wedged past tightly clenched teeth. His heavy face was splotchy with anger. In the background, a woman paced, anxious for a verbal opening of her own.

Danny Young blanched at the onslaught. His homecoming caught him by surprise, but home was still where he wanted to be. In protective custody of sorts. Danny peeked over his shoulders, peered through one of the ruffly white curtains covering the long panes that flanked the front door behind him.

"Have you heard a word I've said?" the man spat.

"Dad, I'm trying to tell you—"

"I didn't think so. Danny, you're rewriting your punishment, and not for the better."

"I'm *sorry*, but it's not my fault. Me and Skippy and Ben—"

"You let Skippy and Ben's folks worry about them. Our job is to look after you. And your job—"

"We were worried sick," the woman said, moving forward in quick, choppy steps. Her arms crossed her body stiffly, as if holding in the illness of which she spoke. "The police have been out looking for you all day. They called in the sheriff's department and contacted the FBI and who knows who else. There are four other pairs of worried parents out there who've spent an entire—"

"Please, Carol. I'm trying to take care of this." Danny's father flapped a hand once and the woman reluctantly backed off, trailing a muttered opinion of one or both male members of her household.

Danny Young embraced his father's anger, his mother's concern, his parents' familiar tirade. It represented life as he'd once known it. Normal life, the highly appropriate reward for having survived the tunnel. He quit listening for the sounds of monsters padding up his family's asphalt drive. He shoved to the back of his mind the dark recollections of his desperate run home and of his concern for Ben. He leaned against the front door frame and shut his eyes.

"Don't you tune us out," his mother warned. "You've got some explaining to do, young man."

"I want him in bed," his father ordered, contradicting and canceling—as usual—his wife's demand. "I've been up half the night as it is. We can talk about this in the morning. And we will."

"Matt, I'm more than a little interested in hearing what he's been doing since this afternoon." Carol Young glanced up at the wall clock. "Excuse me...since yesterday afternoon."

"Right now what's important for all of us is sleep," Danny's father insisted. "I told you it was no big deal. This is a quiet town, Carol. I feel ridiculous now, spending the day with that pushy Upshaw woman and the others. What could we have possibly imagined happening to him that warranted the kind of attention—"

"Skippy got eaten by monsters."

The boy's comment silenced his parents in mid-tirade. His father squinted, his fleshy face accepting one more stern eyebrow line. Danny's mom shifted her weight to one foot, hugged herself tighter. Her eyes behind her oversized glasses turned dark and hard.

Danny wished that the entry hall holding him wasn't so tiny. The air was hot with his parents' proximity. Danny sucked his lips into his mouth and nibbled them thoughtfully while daring himself to continue.

"I'm telling the truth, Mom. Dad. There was a...there were these tiny heads in the bushes, and when we went through the tunnel it was like, like...the moonlight was...and the monster with wings, the toad, it was eating Skippy in the huge field, but when Greg went back to find Tony..."

He let the story peter out. Even if he'd found the right combination of words, it wouldn't have made a difference. He could see by their expressions that he'd lost them.

"Danny, you're burying yourself deeper," his father said, carefully handling each word like an executioner sharpening his axe.

His mother walked away, past the living room and into the small kitchen. She grabbed the wall phone and stretched the cord so she could glare at her son. "What's Skippy's number?"

"Jesus, Carol," her husband whined. "We had to spend the day with the Crenshaws. You want to tuck them in for the night, too?"

Yes. Good idea. Danny searched his brain, eagerly picking out the proper seven-digit sequence. He called it out and his mother dialed.

They'd believe him now; they'd have to. At the very least they'd find that his best friend was still missing, and that would have to prove something. Maybe it wasn't too late to save Skippy now that the adults were involved. Suppose he'd only been unconscious, and not dead. That was possible, wasn't it? They'd know what to do, the parents, the adults. They'd know how to rescue Skippy.

"Hi...Jane? This is Carol Young again. Hate to call you so late, but is Skippy home yet? Un-huh...un-huh. Danny, too. No, everything's fine. Sorry again, but...sure. Bye, now."

Danny knew. Knew even before his mother picked her way slowly back to the entry foyer, head down, arms crossed. She was examining her anger, deciding what size parcels to dole it out and over what period of time.

His father could read her body language as well as Danny. "Well, I guess we've heard enough lies for one night," he rumbled. He moved his big body aside to clear a path straight to the staircase. "We'll talk more tomorrow morning," he promised again.

Danny's mind saw Trevor the way he'd been in the tunnel before *changing.* He shivered, wondering what had returned to the Crenshaw household in the guise of Skippy.

The Young residence was a neat little bungalow, vinyl beige on the outside, trimmed in a seascape shade of blue; crisp white on the inside with brief, bright touches of color for enforced cuteness. But the most important design element, as far as Danny was concerned at the moment, was the layout of the bedrooms: two downstairs, and one all alone up on the second floor.

His lonely bedroom.

Danny felt his folks' cold stares following his climb. Every reluctant footfall took him farther away from the way things had always been. He turned at the staircase's halfway point, his parents now lost in the shadows thrown by the outlandish yellow moonlight He pictured his mother still clasped tightly in her own arms, his father stiff with contained rage.

One of them snapped off the upstairs hall light from downstairs as Danny reached his bedroom doorway. The boy quickly flooded his room with light, first from an overhead, then from a desk lamp. He wished for even more illumination, for a bulb with enough glare to wash away the bright darkness.

Flinging his clothes, he pounced onto his spread and tucked himself under, shielding his body from whatever might be lurking beneath. He grabbed at the drapes by his headboard, pulled them shut to keep out the terrible night.

But it was too late. The creature had found him.

Danny fought to convince himself that he hadn't seen what he knew he had. That he hadn't been discovered by the winged toad that ate Skippy and was now waiting for him outside.

Gliding and waiting.

If he counted slowly to ten...said the Lord's Prayer...recited the Pledge of Allegiance...if he did everything he could think of to shut down his mind for enough time, the hideous reality might dissolve. He would forget everything, the sweating tunnel and what happened to Trevor and that empty sky with the horrible cratered moon.

Mostly, forget the things waiting for him outside.

He shut his eyes tight, yet fought off sleep. If he slept it would get him...the toad...

His rasping gasps smoothed out, tense muscles loosened, and heart slowed. He could hear his parents murmuring downstairs as they prepared for bed. No doubt they were discussing him, throwing blame and manufacturing new rules and regulations that would re-instill the family values of obedience and corrigibility.

That was all right...fine...fair enough. No problem.

A toilet flushed. Water ran. Door clicked shut.

As if far away, he heard, "I don't know, Matt. It just looks odd out there. The sky. It's hard to describe..."

He had no idea what his mother was talking about, and it didn't matter. He was too tired, much too tired to care.

The house settled into a comforting silence. There followed a confusing loss of thought that was probably sleep, but Danny had no way of knowing. There were no troubling dreams. He was oblivious to the progress of time until he became aware of yellow moonlight wedging in under his eyelids.

Now he was awake for sure, blinking in fear and sleepy befuddlement. The room was alive with color; the color that he and Ben and Trevor had brought back with them. Danny jumped up, peeked past his heavy drape and out the window.

The front yard glowed, radiated with a fatal dose of that damned yellow moonlight. From behind the Kelton house across the street he saw the cratered moon itself crawling up the sky. He watched it grow larger, more real by the moment.

And outlined against the yellow moon was the monstrous winged toad. Mesmerized, Danny watched the creature glide across the dark horizon like a plane awaiting landing instructions. It was a nightmare that didn't go away with an arm pinch.

He sprung from bed, ran across his cold floorboards, and flung himself out of the door and down the stairs. It was time to let someone else take over.

The moonlight followed, or maybe it led. Like an invisible spotlight, it whisked his attention to the closed door of his parents' bedroom. He listened for their response to all the noise he'd made madly dashing and stumbling to the lower floor, but none came.

Danny touched the doorknob, but before he could turn it, his attention was drawn by the cool draft tickling his nearly naked behind.

Trembling slightly in his Fruit of the Looms, he walked slowly toward the source of the air. The side door was open, the door connecting attached garage to house. He peeked carefully past the screen, and was further surprised to see that the overhead garage door was also open. Two open-door mysteries, not just one.

His folks owned a two-car garage, but only one car. This particular evening, however, a pair of vehicles shared the space.

The post-midnight summer breeze entered the garage from outside, crossed the room, and nudged the squeaky screen door so that it bumped Danny out of the way. He took several steps back, but could still see all too clearly the unfamiliar of the two parked vehicles.

The ice cream truck's cooling engine seemed not merely to tick, but to actually snap in the cement silence. Danny tried to turn away, but couldn't. He stepped closer, to stand once more in the screened doorway. Another gentle breeze brushed into his face the masculine scents of motor oil and warm rubber.

The vehicle stood on big, bouncy tires like a milk truck from the fifties. Its predominant color had once been white, but it had gone without benefit of a wash for some time. A bright shade of yellow was splashed across the upper half of the side panel. It served as a background for the words *Ice Cream* which were spelled out in letters consisting of rainbow-colored scoops of the stuff: a strawberry *I*, Neapolitan *C*, vanilla *E*...

Danny lightly pushed the screen door and took a tentative step out. He could feel the cool cement floor with one naked, exploring foot. The eye-awakening sensation backed him up, sent him into a slow, dreamy retreat into the house. With only a distracted memory of getting there, he found himself shivering in his underpants in front of his parents' bedroom door.

167

It was true, all of it. He hadn't made anything up, though he wished he had. Now what he had to do was convince *them*. Danny inhaled noisily while collecting his thoughts. Maybe they'd hear the raspy sound of his fear and invite him in. No matter how angry they were, he'd explain, just keep talking. They'd understand. They'd have to.

He surrendered to panic when the screaming started behind him. He prepared to simply collapse and let the monsters take him. He had escaped whatever had eaten Skippy and had outrun the Trevor-thing coming out of the tunnel, but there was a limit to his endurance.

The scream hit him again, less unexpected this time, but equally startling.

Danny blushed as he realized he was hearing the telephone on the wall in the kitchen.

He froze. Listened. Waited for his parents to respond to the sound. He could hear muffled voices behind the closed door that proved the two were awake, but no one came out.

Danny placed a hand on the cool plastic receiver as it trilled a third time. Who'd be calling at this hour?

He picked it up as the phone began its fourth insistent demand for attention. Who...?

He heard only the ragged sound of his own breathing as it entered the phone via the little holes near his mouth and returned to him from the earpiece, creating a closed circuit of terror that welded the receiver to his skull

"Daaany...d'you miss us?"

He knew the voice and realized how relatively unsurprised he was to hear from him.

There were several other voices in the background. "Is that the little asshole that left us behind?" a gruff, deeper voice asked.

The Skippy-voice he'd heard first said, "It's so cool, Danny. You're gonna love it here." It ended in a high, familiar giggle.

Danny stared at the phone, followed the looping cord with his eyes. Thought about how much it resembled a miniature amusement park slide or a corkscrew roller coaster track. It was impossible that this novelty invention should carry sound.

"Hey dickweed," another gruff phone voice contributed. Greg or Tony, it was still hard distinguishing between the two, even in death. "We'll be seeing you and that shitface Ben soon now, y'hear?"

The similar-sounding voice added, "In Ben's case, we're seeing him real soon. Right about now."

The Skippy-thing giggled appreciatively in Danny's ear, a high-pitched purr.

Danny dropped the phone. It rattled off his shin several times in descending arcs, but he barely felt it.

He was staring at his folks' door, where most of the moonlight had gathered. It used to be tan, that door, but now it glowed with every shade of yellow never created.

Knock first, he'd always been told.

Disregarding that good advice, he turned the knob and walked in.

Their lights were off, but who needed lights with yellow moonlight?

He found them coiled tightly together as if wrestling for possession of the mattress. Danny knew he shouldn't be watching. He'd been warned about keeping his distance when that door was closed; now that he'd disobeyed, he knew what it was he was meant not to see.

His father popped up from his position astride Danny's mother. The damp bedsheet wrapped in and out of twisted limbs, his and hers.

A slim leg twitched under him.

Red strands glistened and fell from his father's mouth, splotching the floral sheets. Something black peeked from one vacant eyehole.

His mother said nothing, didn't even try to hide the gory nakedness of her upper torso. Her leg twitched once more, then went limp.

Danny's father ran the back of his hand across his wet lips and wiped off on the sheet.

"Told you it was cool," he said in Skippy's high, enthusiastic voice.

From the garage, Danny could hear the sound of an engine catching, accompanied by another speaker-amplified ditty.

"To Hell you're bound, to Hell you'll go."

The ice cream truck would never leave him, he realized. Not as long as he still had his sanity.

Chapter Thirty-Three

Everything hurt, but not any worse than the day following his last attempt at full-court basketball. Thad staggered from the Escort, making sure he closed the passenger door tight behind him. He hoped Megan locked up. Not that it would make much difference if Albert Durwood wanted in.

Curiously, he wondered if he could have identified the Escort by color if it weren't his. It had been blue before the hellish moonlight washed over it. Now? Anyone's guess. Perhaps an undiscovered shade of green, the effect of yellow moonlight and moth dust coating the blue.

A breeze picked up and tried to plaster Thad to the Ford, but he fought it off for the dubious distinction of confronting a notorious mass murderer.

Albert Durwood wasn't a big man by any means. He reminded Thad of a boy he'd known in high school. He couldn't recall this other boy's name, but would never forget the eyes. Dark and shiny and not all there, those eyes.

Thad had watched the boy with the eyes, all of one-thirty dripping wet, humiliate a school bully in gym class. The bully defined intramural basketball as a contact sport, but so did the boy with the eyes. Not only was he not afraid of his much bigger classmate, but he actually went out of his way to provoke a fight. The bigger boy began leaving the locker room earlier and quieter until the boy with the eyes finally grew tired of the sport. In this way, Thad learned about the unlikelihood of defeating an enemy too crazy to fear consequences.

Too crazy.

Albert Durwood was ready to raise a little hell. You could see it in his watery, eager eyes, the color as wrong as the evening light.

The wind at Thad's back nudged him into the mad crowd. Gaping street people parted like oily water to let him through, most not even noticing his presence. Their eyes rolled, mouths fell, heads lifted to the black sky.

Thad followed their gaze. Where were the stars? The sky was a vacuum, a totality of zero except for the moths fluttering in the breeze.

Something slammed into the side of his head, sending him reeling into a galaxy where the stars were plentiful.

"Thad!"

He waved off his wife while rising—trying to rise—to a sitting position. His mouth tasted of liquid iron: blood, a familiar substance of late. "Stay in the car," he ordered, "and roll up the windows."

Albert Durwood grinned as he leaned in close. The man's entire body shone with the unworldly glow of yellow moonlight. His lips hung loose and wet, face pockmarked like moon soil. "I know so much, Mister Mayor," he said, his hot breath like freshly unearthed mushrooms. "For instance, I know you used to carry the precinct, but you just failed a recall. Meet the new mayor." Two large hands gripped Thad, pulled him to his feet and—

The scene shifts:

He's coming up the steps to a familiar house, middle of the night. The August air hangs as heavy inside as out. Still no lights, but he nimbly dodges several heavy pieces of furniture to find his way stealthily, unerringly to the staircase. He knows where and how to tread upon every riser to exert a minimum of old-wood squeak And once he's found the proper upstairs door, he instinctively knows how far back he can swing it before the hinges protest.

He knows intimately this woman, her face turned and buried in sleep. Could identify her if only by the one small patch of brunette-and-gray hair peeking over the bedsheet.

(Wrong! Hold on, I've never seen her before, his shoved-aside mind screams.) (I'm Thad Crocker, I'm lying here on this big field...)

He looks first at the ball bat in one hand, then at the hand itself. He blinks, tries to concentrate.

(This hand, it's larger than he remembers. It's thicker and rougher, the skin dry and red. It's not mine! he voicelessly shouts.)

He raises the bat to eye level, studies the Louisville Slugger logo he can barely make out in the moonlight coming through one open window.

(Moonlight the color it used to be in the good old days.)

He makes one large hand join its mate in a businesslike grip. He plants both feet in an athletic stance, feels himself smile.

Megan stirs, murmurs something in her sleep, her voice a faintly felt whisper of weakness and bovine contentment.

(Megan? No, not...)

Of course she's content, the bitch. She feels safe on the side of those who plot against him.

No, that doesn't give her enough credit. She leads those who'd destroy him.

The wife and the three.

The three.

(Who? What three?)

The girl, Melinda, the youngest. In the room across the hall. Asleep now, he hopes. Always a sound sleeper till lately.

(Wait. Who am I? I'm Thad Crocker. Who's Melinda and how do I know her? Who's in my head, goddamnit...?)

And Ben, the middle one. Wiry, but slow.

(Ben? No no no that's not right.)

Another who sleeps too sound, like mom and sis. Conspirators always sleep well, secure in their imagined strength. Not like him, the intended victim of their treachery.

Wouldn't they be restless if they knew what he knew; if they could even guess the terrible beauty of the gods of the drains. He knows so much it's frightening.

(No, this is wrong. I'm Thad Crocker, I love my family. Get out get out—)

The one to watch out for is the oldest: Alex. Out for the evening again, of course. Recruiting more tormentors, no doubt. He'll be home soon, and he's the strongest, big for seventeen and much faster than his dull-assed little brother.

Surprise, Alex. Dad's waiting up.

He raises the baseball bat skyward, stretches his thick frame like a runner preparing his body for the race of his life and—

(No! God, no! Wake up, lady, he's going to—)

—whistles it through the air and completes its arc with a gratifying crunch. It's a small sound, but loaded with irreversible results.

Neat. Sweet. Petite. She groans, a mere whisper of response. Coughs sharp and bubbly. Still face-down, she sputters out another small noise that's as discreet as a lady's hiccup.

Again he raises the bat, again he bring it down. The cracking of her skull is rather muffled, not at all what his vivid imagination had constructed. Crunch time is actually rather anticlimactic.

Crunch time. He stifles a laugh.

She gurgles faintly, this scheming bitch wife of his. Her breath stutters like a child about to break out into righteous sobs.

Then it stops.

(Looks a little like Megan, but that's just a mirage; her hair brown like Megan's except where it glistens blackly. Brown? It was gray a moment ago, wasn't it? And her sheet-covered body heavier. Oh, Jesus, if—)

"Mom? Mom?"

This other voice comes from far off, from another room. It's at once tense and embarrassed as his daughter asks her mother to intrude into a nightmare while knowing she's too old to expect such trivial aid.

Melinda has claimed a lot of nightmares lately, but the gods of the drains have explained to him that there are no bad dreams. His scheming daughter's cries are coded messages to bring the rest of the family together in the middle of the night so they can discuss the Daddy situation without raising his suspicions.

Tonight Daddy's talking back, little girl. For years he listened to their careful sarcasm, intercepted their knowing glances, felt their diplomatically phrased criticisms of his job, his drinking, his so-called abuses. For years and years he faced them alone, one against four, and they always won. Their word against his that sent him to jail in the wee hours of loud weekends. It was the authorities working for the wife and kids who held him down: the cops, the social workers, that meddlesome bitch at the women's shelter.

But then came the influential friends of his own, so now it's his turn at bat. He listens for more sounds from his marriage bed and hears nothing, no more goddamned back talk He picks up his instrument of punishment and calls out softly so as not to disturb the middle boy before his time. "It's all right, princess. Daddy's coming."

He hears a deep chuckle of appreciation for his sharp wit and knows where it comes from.

The bathroom drain.

(I'm Thad Crocker, Thad Crocker, Thad Crocker. Get out of my head.)

"Something woke me up," says the small, startling voice from the hallway. Jessie rubs the sleep from her eyes and crawls into the bed with her mother

(No! Not Jessie!)

Thad screamed.

The murderer's eyes were lost. They stared through him but saw nothing. His body odor was sharp, undefinable. Face shiny with sweat.

Thad scooted away, his head swaying erratically, uncontrollably. He tested his clearing vision against a peeling billboard with an obsolete political message. Something crashed into his ribs.

Just as his dentist used to promise, he felt pressure, not pain. Like running a hand under a tap and immediately knowing the water's too hot or too cold. You're not sure which, yet. Just know your system's about to undergo an unpleasant jolt of one kind or another as soon as the nerve endings get around to making out a report.

He couldn't breathe.

Durwood, still grinning, drew back his foot for another body punt to match his initial effort. His eyelids fluttered uselessly, but his foot seemed to work just fine. Durwood was wearing running shoes, the soft soles about the only reason Thad hadn't experienced the memorable sensation of fracturing ribs.

Something bleated, an inhuman sound that slashed the night air. Durwood looked up, posed like a flamingo on one leg.

The sound hurt nearly as much as anything else all evening, but that was because Thad had fallen only a few feet from the Escort. The horn still reverberated in his throbbing skull. He stood slowly, painfully—yes, the old nerve endings were back on the job—and launched himself at the other man.

He couldn't believe what he was doing, the part of Thad's mind that was sitting back and taking notes. He hadn't deliberately tried to harm another human being since the last time he'd duked it out with his brother in junior high—unless the Vern Withers he'd faced earlier counted as human, but Thad rather doubted it.

Megan had given him a chance at survival with the horn blast that had stolen Durwood's attention for a crucial second or two.

Thad whumped into the killer. Both men gasped at the impact. They went down hard, Durwood getting the worst of it as he was sandwiched between the ground and his assailant.

Thad made fists of both hands and pounded away. He inhaled sharply every time contact was made, the cumulative punishment of two fights to the death in one evening taking its toll on hands, lungs and muscles. *Don't faint,* he ordered his ravaged body. It was all over if he lost consciousness. The Fat Lady's last few bars. Dead-Endsville for him, for Megan, for Ben. His fists rose and fell harder and faster.

Durwood covered his face with both hands to absorb the rain of blows, but it was like hiding under a newspaper during a downpour.

Thad continued to grunt in dull pain, the low sounds coming as rhythmically as his pummeling fists. Something hurt, but his body was in too much shock to indicate where these new pain reports were originating.

The crowd stirred. Under the gradually brightening sky, Thad caught the movement. He cringed, expecting the unstable dozens to swoop down upon him and provide tabloid obituary copy not for the faint of heart.

Moths, millions of them, cavorted like dirty snowflakes among the street people who paid no attention. All eyes were firmly fixed skyward.

The motion catching Thad's attention had been several grimy hands pointing, posed like young concertgoers indicating their approval with raised lighters. Following their gestures, Thad found a brand-new moon rising slowly, steadily.

It was pitted with gullies and valleys and scars beyond comprehension. And the color...

A wail broke free, and the sound was picked up, amplified, repeated over and over. In moments, the vast field echoed with ecstatic and confused cries.

"Just like I dreamed," someone sang out in a voice sharp with twang. "Every day, every night. Finally coming true."

"I don't know," replied a woman inappropriately dressed in beaver, voice clad in fear and doubt. "Sure, it's what they promised us, but..."

The moon was an impossibility, a monstrosity. Thad's muscles locked rigid. No longer able to stay astride Durwood, he slid off, his insides loose. Fell to the ground and waited to die.

As one man fell, another rose. Albert Durwood's eyes were alive once more, gleaming like hot charcoal. He spat once, expelling a tooth ahead of a wet trail of saliva and blood.

"I knew it, I knew it, I knew it," the madman whispered. "The gods of the drains. Here. Now." Durwood's broken face split further into a broad grin.

Insanity, Thad realized, can be a valuable gift. He wished not to see with such dreadful clarity himself.

Chapter Thirty-Four

One two three, curl.

It was as if Ben had planned the whole thing, choreographed his defense like the George Balanchine of survival. First he'd slammed the bathroom door on what remained of his advancing friends. That had gained him a second or two before the two crashed through, enough time to hop onto the window ledge and claw the screen away with his fingers. Unseen wire stabbed under his nails, the worst pain he could even imagine enduring. Swinging the screen like a ball bat, he let the charging Greg-creature wear it like an oversized necklace beneath its rapidly changing skull. That Keystone Kops routine bought Ben another couple seconds. He ducked his head and pitched the upper half of his body out the window, his lower half anchored to the sill by the seat of his pants. Hearing more than seeing the still-advancing abominations, he curled his legs against his chest, then pistoned them outward, only his strong stomach muscles bracing him on the sill. His feet caught something in the bathroom, something that crackled, yielding squishy softness like the runny guts of breakfast eggs. Ben grabbed his knees on the rebound, curled, and pulled his legs out the window to join the rest of his body.

One two three, curl. The Ben Crocker Twenty-Second Workout for Cardiovascular Fitness and Monster Avoidance.

Now he was fighting off hysteria while grabbing the slanting roof over his front porch. He couldn't help remembering all the times he and his friends had slithered out onto that trouble spot until his dad chased them away. Of course, if his folks wanted to yell at him now for being out there, he hadn't an objection in the world.

The voice in the drain, that hadn't been his father's. Couldn't have been. It was just another monster trying to trick him, like those things with the round black heads weren't the Luckinbill brothers. Not anymore.

Of course, it was possible that the monsters had hurt his father before stealing his voice, just like they'd hurt Greg and Tony first. Maybe they'd even...

Angrily, he flicked at a tear forming in one eye. No time for that.

The Tony-thing was coming through the bathroom window. He tanned better than his older brother, that was the only way Ben could identify who the first monster climbing through was pretending to be. He—*it*—was still wearing shorts and had enough leg remaining for identification purposes, but the limb was changing rapidly. It was crooked, gnarled, like a walking stick you might find in the woods. The skin was torn, sometimes in big chunks, the open wounds clogged with a sticky, yellow fluid. Something black and leathery like Tony's new head peeked through where the bones should have been. Thin, black tubes cut through the skin, writhing, twisting.

Now the rest of the body came through the bathroom window after Ben. The broken thing that had once been Tony's head dangled like a cowl from the back of the creature's neck. The new skull had red eyes that resembled buttons haphazardly glued onto a scarecrow. It was a wolfish shade of red staring back, the eyes reflecting the yellow moonlight fuzzying the night air.

When the creature's head lifted to find the strange sky, Ben used the distraction wisely. He hopped up and grabbed the main roof, just barely within extended arm reach, and pulled himself toward the house's highest point. The fascia crackled and groaned like the spine of an old man who reluctantly tussles with heavy grandkids, but the wood held.

In that split second with his back turned and body dangling helplessly against gravity and old wood, Ben knew that he wasn't going to be able to shimmy himself up. Knew he'd hang there like fresh meat on a hook to be slashed into bite-sized morsels. He could sense the monsters grinning, grasping.

Climbing from lower roof to big roof was a feat he'd attempted unsuccessfully on countless occasions, but this time it came as natural as breathing—and every bit as fundamental to his survival. Just up, up, up! His arms and shoulders and legs had never felt stronger.

He could now look directly down and see both monsters shuffling around on the lower roof only feet below him. But if he could climb, they could climb. Ben desperately scanned the rooftop.

The Millers lived next door; he could see the glow of indoor light indicating that the curious sights and sounds from their neighbor's place had pulled them from bed, but he was too high to further draw their attention. The angle was wrong.

The Geralds on the other side owned a taller house, but Ben was hidden from their view by the slope of the Crocker roof. No help there.

The trees in his own front yard obliterated a good view of the Dunlap and Ames residences across the street. Too bad. Through the leaves, Ben could see the lights on at both houses.

The entire town seemed awake, despite the late hour. Now that he thought about it, Ben had heard the distant wail of sirens for the last several minutes of his wild dash home. He'd also heard nervous voices commenting on the yellow light from a porch the next block over. His stomach twitched as he debated whether he'd have been better off stumbling into the first lit doorway he'd passed. At the time, his need for his own parents had been so strong that no other assistance would do, but what if...

No time for what-ifs, he chided himself. All that mattered was saving himself. At least he had what seemed like miles of pitching rooftop to use. It was Pee-Wee's Playhouse up there, with chimneys and nooks and subroofs all over the place if he needed them.

But if he was worried about the Luckinbill brothers—and indeed he was—they no longer seemed all that concerned about him. Their attention was held by the night sky, locked onto the slowly rising moon.

And no wonder.

It was like waking up and seeing Saturn and all its rings bobbing big as a beach ball in a backyard birdbath. Like watching rain shooting skyward. Like finding the sun in the driver's seat of your folks' car or a handful of stars, bright and hard, dancing on the front porch.

Ben plopped down where the roof peaked. Had to or he would have fallen off, the way his muscles twitched and jumped.

One of the rooftop monsters turned and looked up at him. Ben could no longer tell which Luckinbill brother the creature had once imitated, and would never again be able to make the distinction.

"Thank you, son," it said. "Thanks for opening the door."

It spoke in his father's voice.

Ben could only think of Greg and Tony and Skippy and Trevor and his mom and dad, lost forever.

Ben Crocker: lost forever.

So lost that he barely heard the fascia groan as one Luckinbill brother pulled himself onto the main roof and crawled up the shingled peak toward him.

Chapter Thirty-Five

The moonlight froze Albert Durwood's face into a mask of a maniacal snowman. His cold eyes flashed with a color that wasn't in the spectrum. Lips barely moving, his voice rumbled from deep within his chest. "The gods of the drains are nearly in," he said, moving toward the fallen Thad.

Except for the occasional thistle, the soft grass under Thad's prostrate body made for an acceptably comfortable bed. So tempting to just sleep and forget.

Now a familiar voice prickled him with new urgency; Megan, out of the car and heading his way, ordering him back onto his feet, to run, to escape. He did nothing.

Albert Durwood half-turned to swat her to the ground with one swipe of a thick forearm.

Thad's hand shot out and wrapped itself around the killer's nearest leg. He twisted and Durwood stumbled, shifted his weight onto the capturing hand and sent his free foot crashing into Thad's ribs. With an "*ooph*" the fight left Thad, his feeble adrenaline surge easily consumed by the fire of pain.

The crowd, which had been milling about in dazed confusion, offered up a few hoots of approval amidst a general buzz of nervous concern.

Thad caught a flurry of activity as the short, stout woman in ragged fur worked her way out of the crowd to put herself between Megan and the killer. Squatting next to Thad's glassy-eyed wife, the woman glared fearlessly at Durwood looming overhead. "You're special, all right, but I seen your kind of special before." She sniffed. "Not better than others, just stronger. Been a good long time since I backed down from a so-called strong man like you."

Thad struggled to a sitting position. He watched in dull surprise as Durwood studied this thoroughly unexpected challenge from one of his own.

"I'm with ya, Melba," mumbled a one-armed black man who, despite his words, made little effort to stand out from the crowd.

"C'mon, leave 'er alone, why dont'cha," coarsely pitched in an unseen female. A few others added words of nervous support.

"You forgettin' what they done ta us?" someone shouted.

"Fuck 'em," added another.

The street people broke up into murmuring cliques of indecision.

Megan propped herself on one elbow, supported by one of Melba's broad, scarred hands. Megan patted the hand and smiled at her rescuer.

Durwood's brooding scowl shifted from Melba to Megan to the crowd and back. Then his doubts seemed to dissolve into an accommodating shrug, as one might wrap up internal debate over whether to punish a house-wetting puppy by ignoring the offense.

He turned his attention back to Thad, yanking him to his feet and pulling him close to his own flushed face. Durwood's eyes flashed pale and dark and colorless and pale again.

Thad made a soft fist and thumped it off of the other man's chest.

Durwood never noticed. "I did it, Mister Mayor," he hissed. "I opened the way, and your kid let them in. Even better than killing you and wifey is letting you all live with the gods of the drains."

Thad couldn't pry his attention from that disfigured moon overhead with its gouged craters and blunt shadows. You could go insane just trying to guess the disgusting, throbbing color.

Durwood's attention was drifting elsewhere as well, a loose smile working at the sides of his mouth. He loosened his grip on Thad's collar, letting him slip once more to the ground.

Turning to the crowd, he said in a voice low enough to cause the others to strain. "You doubters and second-guessers out there, let me show you why you're on the right path."

Another hush fell over the crowd as Durwood cut through it to stare intently at the emptiness of more fields and pastures and scraggly open spaces to the south, the interstate somewhere in the unseen, unheard distance. He cocked his head.

Thad painfully crawled the dozen feet to his wife. Their hands touched and she smiled, her dark eyes shimmering unnaturally in the yellow light. The street woman Melba clenched Megan's waist protectively, Thad's nostrils twitching with the musky sweat-scent of the unwashed woman.

"He's going to be all right," Megan whispered.

Her willful confidence nearly broke his heart. "Of course he is," Thad agreed, but he had to choke back his tears. If anything happened to Ben...

Albert Durwood raised his hands above his head. A summer night breeze rustled the clover and weeds, but under that gentle sound came another, a mechanical hum that could be coming from anywhere on the horizon.

At least thirty pairs of eyes scanned the broad, glowing expanse with intense and varied expectations.

The throaty sound gradually gained in volume until it turned into a car engine. The crowd gasped—probably with no idea why—when a pair of headlights poked twin holes in the yellow light.

Durwood glanced over his shoulder to smirk directly at Thad. "Watch this, Mister Mayor. Here's what you're dealing with."

He'd passed out once he reached the cruiser. Nothing dramatic, more like a nap that simply had to be taken despite all his responsibilities. When he came to and tried to raise assistance on the radio, he found he was alone in a world reduced to white noise static and a right leg that seemed to be burning to smoldering ash. Except for one tiny puncture ruining a pair of blues, everything looked normal down there, but his nerve endings knew differently.

He didn't remember starting his engine or driving out of Irv Coy's soybean field. His tires, straying far from the corky road that had wheeled him in, bogged down in spring mud that tore at his transmission and his patience. It was the protesting whine of his engine that brought him out of his latest pain stupor to find yet another corky road preceding him out of one desolate field and into another.

Tom Luckinbill groaned. He had no more strength for this. His single-minded goal was to find his boys, and he had little confidence that this road would get him wherever he had to be. He jumped, then swore as grandly as his weakening condition would allow when his grille snapped up a length of barbed wire and whipped it at the windshield.

Shadowy movement in the distance might have been grazing cattle, but it became a ragged crowd. One lone figure stood apart from the others, hands raised like an aircraft carrier deckhand bringing home a fighter jet.

It was a figure he knew. He had no idea how Albert Durwood fit into all of this and didn't care except that the killer deliberately stood between him and his boys. He let his pent-up fury make his next move for him. He stomped the pedal, sending a lightning bolt of new pain up his leg and into his spine. Tom gnashed his teeth against a faint reflex, and waited for the powerful 424-cc engine to lunge into the man controlling the road.

It didn't happen. The cruiser's powerful engine roared as commanded, but his speedometer never flickered from its rough and tumble forty-eight miles an hour.

He swung the wheel to the right without even looking to see where he might be directing the car. Knew it didn't matter, that he was going to follow the freshly laid road no matter what he did.

The engine hum turned into a rumble. The headlights found the street people, sent them reeling blindly for nonexistent cover. Tires threw dirt as the patchy land transformed into a road leading straight to Albert Durwood.

The murderer stood stone-still, arms raised, fists clenched at the night.

Thad sprang to his feet, praying his adrenaline tank had been sufficiently refueled. He tucked in his head and charged. He could hear Megan's sharp cry of warning, saw disoriented street people squirming out of his way, heard the deep, dangerous roar of the approaching car, smelled gasoline and rubber and engine heat.

The rumble decreased in pitch a notch as the cruiser slipped into a lower gear going into its stop mode.

Not yet! his mind screamed.

Then he was where he had to be, the palms of his hands lying flat against the sweaty-hot fabric of the mass murderer's shirt, pressing, pressing. He shoved with all he had left.

"Yes!" the driver shouted as he watched Durwood's statue-pose break with the help of another man riding his back. Tom's foot went once more to the accelerator, but he was stopped, nearly paralyzed by another lightning bolt of searing pain. It was as if his wounded leg was holding him back.

He grunted in ornery obstinacy, pounded through the excruciating pain, found the pedal, slammed it south, and felt the car instantly respond. His hood shuddering with uncontrollable speed, he aimed for the off-balance Durwood and the man on his back.

"Get off him," Luckinbill muttered. In another second there'd be two corpses rather than one, not that that possibility would stop him from breaking the control of the son of a bitch keeping him from his boys.

Durwood's body stuttered, arms flailing for balance. Thad kept pushing, pushing, making sure the killer had no time to reassert control.

Thad closed his eyes and heard...his wife scream...the cruiser's engine gun with new speed...the street people giggle, snarl, moan and bleat in joy, hate, fear, confusion.

Durwood was a maverick stallion with a saddle. He frothed with rage and wild fear, bucking for freedom, but Thad rode him with the grip of a man out of hope: a toss would be more fatal than the ride.

His ankles were stung by plowed-up dirt from the careening car. His chest vibrated from the growling engine almost on top of them. Now or never.

He dived to his right, instantly wondering why he assumed the cruiser wouldn't do the same to avoid collision with the pair of them. What a god-awful irony, for Thad to be the only casualty.

Hitting the ground hard, he turned in time to see the cruiser front-ending the killer, breaking and flinging him into the night sky.

Durwood bleated once, a short and insignificant sound, before whumping face-down to the tire-churned soil. Something cracked: bones, lots of them. A fine and highly localized blood mist followed Durwood's trajectory. Thad felt a few drops on his face, but the red rain ended before it really began, like a little precipitation squeezed from a minor cloud.

The sky exploded, became instant daylight shimmering with tornado colors. The crowd yammered in frustration, confusion, terror.

"Get in."

Thad blinked. Tom Luckinbill was motioning him toward his police cruiser. The vehicle's twisted front bumper dripped liquid darkness.

Something grabbed his arm and Thad cried out, shrank away.

"It's me, love."

Megan, her face crinkled with pain, pale with fear. He let her steer him toward the police car, both of them limping. Her touch was cool against his bruised arm, his bruised body.

He turned to say something to her, but she was gone. He swiveled his head frantically and found her with Melba, the street woman. Megan was pulling on her ratty coat, pulling her toward the cruiser, but the woman was leaning the other way like a dog that didn't want to be walked. Melba shook her head, but patted his wife's forearm as if apologizing for the rejection.

"What was that all about?" he asked when she came back. He had to scream to be heard above the din.

"She saved my life. I wanted her to come with us, but she wouldn't."

Thad shrugged, pushing his wife into the cruiser. It smelled of old coffee and spent cigarettes. Recycled fast-food bags and wrappers and Styrofoam cups and ketchup packets covered the seats and floor mats. The radio growled, with electric noise reeking of danger.

"She also said I reminded her of Tina," Megan said. She huddled between the two men, all three sharing the front seat.

Tom thumped the transmission out of park and the police car roared over the weedy ground. He punched the steering wheel, emitting short belches of horn sound to scatter ragged, dazed pedestrians.

"She saved my life, and I'd have never noticed her on the streets." Megan sounded like she was talking in her sleep. Dreamily, she stroked a hand that had been rubbed raw, most likely by their encounter with Vern Withers.

Thad's body shot him pain signals at every dip as Luckinbill took the scarred landscape at a suspension-wrecking speed.

Megan kept talking, always talking. "We stopped it just in time, Thad. That must be why things are clearing up nicely now. Isn't it starting to look nice out again, Thad?"

She was babbling, but Thad didn't care. If he could sleep, if he could forget for just a half-hour...

"Look," she cried.

She was pointing toward the creepy road that had led them to the field. It was trembling as if being hit by an earthquake of impressive magnitude.

Great, Thad thought. A grand finale right off the Richter scale. About all the town needed to finish off a truly remarkable day.

"I'm not taking that road," Tom Luckinbill said. "Roads like that you gotta stay off of. Funny things happen." The police chief's speech was solemn, thick, like a maudlin drunk. He rubbed his thigh where his pants were torn and further marred by a few splotches of blood.

"It's melting," Megan said.

A melting, shimmering road. Like the Wicked Witch of Oz. It was nearing invisibility now, rough patches of thistle bleeding through the remaining mirage.

The sky seemed to be clearing up, too. The ghastly light was thinning out quickly everywhere. Thad leaned out the open passenger window.

"What is it?" Megan asked, her tired voice filling with alarm.

"Nothing." That was the point. Nothing in the sky but stars. Nothing to be seen of that damned moon until he leaned out far enough to catch a glimpse of it falling into a line of trees on the horizon.

"Hope to hell this rough ground doesn't rip out my transmission," Tom said. "Least not till we get to your place. That's where I was headed when that goddamned Durwood grabbed me. It's where my boys are, at your place." Then he added pointedly, or so it seemed to Thad, "No thanks to that young one of yours."

"Ben's home?" Thad cried as if remembering his son for the first time.

"Yeah, probably," the police chief said in a flat, glum tone. "I mean, Greg and Tony will be there, so..."

The nightmare was ending.

At one point, Tom veered his car sharply away from some very unusual-looking plants. The leaves were tumbling inward like imploding buildings or a high-speed film showing the effects of water deprivation on vegetation.

The car ride smoothed out when they found trustworthy pavement; real, made-in-Cleary cement located a few minutes from the Crocker residence on Merryside Drive.

All three jumped when flashed from behind by strobing red and blue lights.

"Maybe we should stop," Megan said, flicking a thumb at the county cruiser in the rearview mirror.

Tom jerked his head from side to side. "I'm getting my boys. Sheriff Gattis, he can kiss my ass for all the help he's been."

Merryside seemed to be hosting a midnight sleep-over. Several pajama-clad people tried to flag down the cruiser, but Tom Luckinbill either didn't see them or took perverse pleasure in watching dignified citizens dodge his unyielding tires.

If they hadn't known the precise address of the Crocker residence, they could have just driven by till they saw the action.

"I told my guys and Gattis to meet us here," Tom said. He scrunched up his face at a uniformed officer in a flat-brimmed hat. He was directing traffic. "Highway Patrol. So Joanie did it. Well, shit. That's a complication."

It looked to Thad like the police chief had called in everyone but the 82nd Airborne. He counted three ambulances, two fire trucks, and a greater quantity and variety of squad cars than the peaceful little town had ever seen off an Independence Day parade route. No wonder the gawkers were out in full force. This day and evening was set to become a Cleary legend, Thad hadn't the slightest doubt.

The car squealed to make a sharp left and roared up the Crocker driveway at 618 Merryside.

Chapter Thirty-Six

It was fading now, that magnificent globe in the sky. The light, once so indescribably hopeful, was dying. With its death came the birth of new ideas to Melba McCann.

No...that wasn't entirely true. Her thoughts had started clearing at about the time the madman Durwood was harassing that poor couple.

The madman.

Do the insane recognize the insane? Her ability to truly see Durwood shone like a light in her private darkness.

Melba sometimes felt she had important knowledge in her clenched fist, but that every time she opened it the wisp of wisdom fluttered away. Or that she was awakening from a beautiful dream to the realization that her memories were dissolving, and the harder she struggled to retain them the faster they went, until the morning left nothing but the recollection of having dreamt.

She had no idea how long she posed in that weed-choked field, her closed eyes aimed at the dark heavens. Her muscles were stiff, arms tight at her sides. She knew nothing of the murmuring, sobbing, whispering mob around her, not at first. She swarmed with thoughts, ideas, philosophical snippets that tickled her mind before fluttering away.

Occasionally she'd say to herself, *So that's why I acted like that*; or she'd think, *The reason the voices could affect me and not others had to do with my emotional state because of...because of...*

And then the knowing would be whisked away, leaving her with nothing but a tantalizing scrap or two of insight.

"It gonna be okay, Melba honey. We goin' back with 'em. We all goin' back and life be so good for all us."

She opened her eyes. The moon was still lowering, but quicker now, like a balloon that had been blown up but not tied off. The normal sky with the normal stars caught and bounced back sudden flashes of color from distant emergency vehicles. Sirens continued to wail from several directions as they converged on the town on the other side of the park.

"What now?" she asked. She was lost, but felt calmer than ever before.

Her new friend Lucas pointed his only arm, pointed it at a place at the edge of the field where the land formed a slight rise under a dreary billboard. "We goin' home," he said.

She noticed the opening in the hill at the same time as many of the others. Until that moment, the crowd had shared a stunned and aimless silence in reaction to the harsh swiftness of recent developments. But with the discovery of the tunnel, all that changed.

"They waited for us," said a man with a raspy voice.

"No no no, it's all wrong," sobbed an excitable woman with dark teeth, but she advanced as quickly upon the tunnel as the others.

Melba McCann came closer, too.

"Faster," someone shouted to no one in particular. "It gonna disappear like the yellow moon. And when it gone, it ain't be never coming back no more."

Melba stopped in front of a red, greasy bundle drawing fat flies. It could no longer frighten her, that bundle. Could no longer terrorize that nice young couple, either. One blood-clogged eye glared up at her, raged on into eternity.

"Durwood was the one they needed. The rest of us were just tuned in to the same frequency, sort of."

"He was a great man," her friend Lucas said reverently.

"I never trusted him." She sniffed, not sure if she trusted her own words. "Man was a monster."

"Didn't say he was a *good* man. Got us that yellow moon, though."

"Yeah," she admitted, almost wistfully. "Got us the yellow moon."

Lucas said, "Lots of famous men, great men, wouldn't wanna invite 'em in for dinner, but it's what they 'ccomplish, not what they are that's important. Now come on, 'fore we miss it, Melba."

She could no longer see the tunnel on account of the crowd clustered around it.

"Goddamnit, move," someone growled. "Go in or stay out, but don't block it like that."

"You going, Lucas?" she asked. She didn't know the answer, which surprised her. She already missed her fabulous mind-reading gift.

He stared. Blinked, like he'd never considered the question. "Well…" He pinched his nose to clear it, rubbing finger and thumb on his once-white shirt. "See any reason for stayin' behind, Melba?"

A few of the ragged people were leaving the tunnel area. Heads down, they dragged themselves toward the distant road.

At least she had options. "I have a daughter," she said slowly.

Lucas looked away, pivoted a toe in the loose dirt. "Uh-huh. What she think of you, Melba? What she think of your mind?"

The tunnel was as hidden by the ragged mass as a quarterback by his huddle. Angry voices were breaking out again, one man threatening another for taking too long to decide. Glass shattered as an empty bottle was converted to a tool of persuasion.

"You be crazy not to go," a voice shouted to appreciative laughter.

"Tina thinks I'm not right," Melba admitted. "Thinks I need a hospital, doctors, medication."

"Do you?"

An old man cried out, "Hurry up! It's nearly gone."

Melba pulled herself closer to the center of activity, her tired feet crackling upon the brittle forms of dying moths. She was painfully aware of her age, of her earthly weariness, of the hunger gnawing her from within. She fell in step with the crowd, let it jostle her into a rough line still forming in front of the tunnel.

Line-forming was a skill that no one on the crusty fringes of society could do without. They'd all done time in food lines, unemployment lines, lines for surplus cheese and used shoes and overcoats.

Now she caught a glimpse of the tunnel. It was a muddy, neutral shade of gray, any real color bleeding away fast. Dark weeds poked through as its solidity—its very reality—continued to fade.

She turned to Lucas, queuing behind her. "To answer your question, I'm part sane, part not."

A tall man in front of her, actually a boy with big hands and big hair, chuckled. "Lady, you're talking about all of us. But which is the sane and which's the 'not'? Answer that and you're cured."

That was the trick, all right. Could be the solution was on the other side, no use denying it. Least it seemed they wanted her over there. Same couldn't be said of this side.

The big-haired man was next. He clapped once his gloved hands with the fingers cut out to gain the attention of the crowd. "This is how you do it," he said. "Without a second thought." He turned to Melba and winked, flexed his knobby knees, and jumped into the darkness. It looked like he was simply going to crash into the hillside, but the feeble tunnel was still strong enough to swallow him whole.

"Don't do it!" the excitable woman with the dark teeth cried, but far too late.

Someone cursed the sobbing woman, and she replied, horrified, "There's no turning back. You go there, you're gone. Forever. Good or bad...forever."

The crowd for once fell silent.

"No shit," someone finally mumbled.

"What if it's worse there than here?" the woman with the dark teeth wanted to know.

"Impossible," the mumbling man replied.

It was Melba's turn.

The tunnel shimmered. Seemed to be winking at her, but most likely it was merely dying, the way a car in critical need of a tune-up will death-rattle when the ignition's cut.

"Decision time, Melba." The voice came from a soft-spoken man in a plaid business suit. She'd met him in the Cleary jail, same place she'd met Lucas. He appeared to be well-fed, and his suit looked expensive, but it was imbedded with grime as if he'd lived and slept in it for a month. Melba knew he collected toilet paper rolls, which he stored in a denim knapsack over one round shoulder.

"I'm thinking," she snapped.

"No time," Lucas replied.

When she took hold of her friend's one remaining hand, he broke into a gap-toothed grin. "Together?" His brown eyes were smeared a sickly yellow from an unspecified liver ailment.

"Your life will be much better over there," she said softly. "I can feel it."

He seemed to find the truth in her eyes. "I goin' alone, ain't I?"

She squeezed his hand. "My Tina needs me."

"I know."

She smiled, tried to. "Then you know more than I do. I'm not sure of anything, Lucas. And I can no longer hear you when you're not speaking."

"So what," someone shouted. "That power's waiting for us over on the other side. We'll be like gods over there. Not like here at all."

"We just gonna talk about it, or what?" someone exploded. "Get going or get the fuck out of the way, lady."

Like gods.

"Go," she whispered.

She stepped out of line and watched her friend until there was nothing more to see.

With eyes closed, she tried to picture him, tried to see him in his new world. It would be unbelievably alien over there, like nothing even imaginable on this side. It might be horrible, but no worse than where

Lucas came from. She waited for something, for some kind of message from him, for the faintest mind-tickle to assure her he was well.

Nothing.

She sighed. Ambling off for uncharted territory of her own, she felt not the slightest twinge of guilt at having sent her friend forever into the unknown.

She'd walk until she found Tina.

"But no hospitals," she grumbled to herself. "I may be insane, but I'm not crazy."

Chapter Thirty-Seven

One of his boys was waiting for him on the roof of the house, feet dangling limp. Tom squinted. "Tony, that you?"

He saw Megan Crocker rush up her porch, attack her front door and disappear within. Despite the crowd noise, he could hear her thunder up the stairs. Okay, so the one on the roof was her own.

Tom took several steps into the front yard and nearly tripped over something. A crackly shell, Like snakeskin, only much larger. Two of them. He scraped his feet on the grass, leaving sooty smears.

"Ben," he called out to the boy still dangling overhead. "My boys, Tony and Greg, headed this way. You seen them yet?"

The boy didn't move much. Just stared off into the night sky. The *normal* night sky, right as Cleary, Ohio. No more of this weird moonlight shit.

"Ben?" Tom had little patience for the so-called friend who'd abandoned his sons. The kid was lucky things had turned out all right, or he'd be in hot water about now.

Megan was poking her head out one window now and waving her boy toward her. He didn't seem to know she was there.

Tom raised his voice, cupping his hands over his mouth. "Ben, come on, you little shit. Where are Greg and Tony? I need answers."

Still staring straight ahead—ignoring his mother behind him—the boy pointed to a spot on the ground near where Tom was standing.

He looked. Saw nothing but those curious burnt-out shells. A few of the neighbors were also examining the blackened things.

Some woman held her mouth and threw up between her fingers into the mayor's rhododendrons.

Something he'd have to investigate, those strange shells. But first he had a lot of catching up to do with his sons. He'd never had the proper time, but he was about to change all that. Next time those two went to Waylock Park, they'd go with their old man. Hell, he still had a few things he could show them out on the old ball diamond, proper sliding techniques and the like.

He heard his name being called. Sounded urgent, but it wasn't Greg or Tony so he ignored it.

Another scream lit the pre-dawn. He filed the sound away. Plenty of time later to investigate.

After he found his boys.

Epilogue

The parade of news vans still followed him around town, but the reporters kept a slim distance these days. Resentful scrutiny replaced shouted questions that all parties knew would be ignored.

Tom Luckinbill could hear the doorbell gonging behind the chintzy front door. It was a deep, hollow sound that completely overpowered the modest bungalow. Through the door's single glass pane he watched the soft woman shuffle slowly toward him. He glanced over one shoulder so she wouldn't see him watching her looking out at him.

The media army was much smaller these days, offering the possibility that the town's story would eventually be forgotten by the outside world.

He could hope.

The door creaked open, the woman evidently satisfied that it was a friend who stood on her cement stoop, and indeed it was.

They both had so few friends these days.

A heavyset man with an oversized tape recorder moved onto the woman's tidy lawn as the doors opened. He held out the mike like an offering to both of them. "Chief Luckinbill? If you and Mrs. Withers would like to comment—"

"I told you before about trespassing," Tom said mildly. The look in his eyes didn't match the innocuous tone of voice.

The tubby reporter stopped as suddenly as if the ground had opened before him. In accompaniment to his retreat, he mumbled something about his responsibility as a journalist and Tom's as a public servant. Curbside once again, he glared back with his fellow press hounds.

Tom apologized to the woman in the doorway.

"Not your fault," she replied. She turned and walked wordlessly back into the house, as if knowing he'd follow.

Tom shut the door behind him. The dark house closed in with an abundance of knickknacks and shin-smashing furniture. At least it was air-conditioned; there would have been no air movement in the still confinement without it.

"I was in the bathroom," Laura May mumbled.

He followed her into the kitchen and planted himself in a vinyl-backed chair. Avocado chickens scuttled around yellow haystacks on her busy wallpaper. Bright animal magnets clung to the knocked-about white refrigerator. Their electromagnetic jaws and paws held recipes, newspaper clippings, coupons, various things of perceived value to the shapeless woman.

"I'm waiting," she said.

He sat up stiffly, at first thinking she was conveying her impatience with his visit. Then he understood, and nodded. "That's good," he said simply.

Her colorless lips were set in a grim line. Purple pouches under dull eyes documented the restless nights.

Tom figured he must look similarly disheveled these days, but couldn't remember the last time he'd sneaked a peek at a mirror to find out.

He touched her hand on the table top, and hoped she wouldn't take it wrong. It had no doubt been a while since someone other than Vern had expressed such familiarity.

She didn't pull away, but asked if he wanted coffee.

He nodded, figuring the task would give her the excuse she needed to break contact.

Bustling at her stove, she said, "You've been good to me, Tom. I appreciate it."

The phone rang in another room. She stood with one hand reaching for her hot-water kettle, turned to stone until the caller gave up.

He said, "Get an answering machine, Laura May. I got one a week or so ago. After a while you don't even hear the ringing anymore. You return the calls you want, when you want. The rest of them can all go to hell."

She offered a wan smile to go with the colorful mug she set before him. After spoon-dribbling in a weak amount of instant coffee, she added hot water from the kettle.

Three talking cows and a hayseed farmer. It seemed to Tom that cartoon mugs were the lowest form of humor, and he hated instant coffee, but he sipped and smacked his lips in feigned appreciation.

He'd visited Laura May Withers four times in the last eleven days, and had forced himself to drink weak instant coffee in novelty mugs each time. Today it tasted oddly metallic: decaffeinated, on top of its other shortcomings.

She sat across from him with her own cup in hand. "Tom, you're being here is what's gotten me through this ordeal, so far. The way you sit with me and explain things I couldn't possibly understand on my own...I can't say enough." She shrugged, as if to prove her closing words.

"You're doing the right thing," he told her. His voice was soothing, the tone of a law enforcement officer talking a jumper off a ledge. That's how he felt about the woman across from him: that he alone was keeping her on firm ground.

"I went through all that you're going through," he said. "I know how rough it is, but life really will get better. The secret's knowing that what I'm telling you's the truth."

Laura May played with the spoon on the table in front of her, pointing it at her guest, sliding it closer, sliding it farther away. "It's kind of comforting," she said. "The waiting, I mean. Gives me time to think."

"Of course it does. That's exactly the right way to feel." Tom patted the woman's rough hand. He felt so close to her, having experienced much her same pain before his own fog of confusion had lifted.

He sipped again while she did the same. They slurped in unison, noisily, as if mutually avoiding companionable silence.

She set her mug down and smiled. "Vern was never like this. Sitting with me, drinking coffee. Talking. My mom and me, we did this kind of thing all the time, but she died seven years ago."

Tom nodded thoughtfully, unsure how to respond. "Well," he said after a pause, "I should be getting back."

Rising quickly, they barked their chairs together on the linoleum.

"Thanks for the coffee," he said, and immediately winced at the insight that too much appreciation would get him more of the same next visit.

Laura May misread his sour expression and asked him how the leg was doing.

He thought about it, put all of his weight on the injured limb and pivoted. "Hey," he said. "Looks like I'm all cured."

"You didn't seem to be limping when you walked through the house." She sounded tired, like she was only talking to be polite. Confirming his impression, she added, "I have to get back to the bathroom, Tom. Sorry."

"Oh, sure," he said. "No problem. Everything's going to turn out fine. I only stopped by to make sure you still trust me."

He opened the front door and peeked out cautiously.

"They still there?" Laura May asked.

He nodded.

"What are we going to do, Tom?"

Having spotted him at the door, the reporters gestured and chattered to spread the minor news flash among themselves.

"Ignore them," he said. "All we can do, Laura May. They'll get tired of the town eventually."

Something else caught his eye, and he had the wild and dangerous impulse of drawing his gun. But it was some other round-faced kid on a bike coasting past the small crowd by the news vans. Fortunately for the young bicyclist, he wasn't the little bastard who'd tried to take Tony and Greg from him.

Laura May Withers shut and locked her front door immediately upon the exit of her only living friend. She watched the men by the vans nudge each other as Tom moved into camera range. A couple of the braver ones tagged along for half a block before the police chief turned and froze them with an icy stare before opening the door of his cruiser.

Laura May managed both a smile and a frown, as unsure of her emotions now as she'd been for the past couple weeks. Her days would begin under a black cloud of depression that lifted with the exhilarating acceptance of what she knew to be true. Then panic would set in as her thoughts turned deeper...too deep.

The first several days brought cards and letters and flowers and casseroles from people she barely knew. She'd never realized the connection between food and death before the bean dishes and baked goods and deli trays came pouring in from so many neighbors and curious acquaintances.

The funeral arrangements had been easy with all the help she received. She had only to nod at the proper time when asked about caskets or flowers. Oftentimes she didn't know why she was nodding, but the response seemed to advance the intricate process.

There was an awfulness to the entire process of death management that actually entertained her in a bizarre and unforgivable fashion. She'd vaguely wondered at times how a loved one gets to his resting place, how each step is handled: the obituary, death certificate, funeral service, casket and stone, plot and interment. Now she knew, sort of.

It was only now, two weeks later, when she had no more decisions to make, that things were getting difficult. Vern was gone, truly gone, at least in the physical sense. She was having problems accepting that, and was still foggy as to the actual circumstances of his passing, beyond knowing that the Crockers were unpardonably responsible.

She wasn't the only one left sketchy on the details. All of Cleary, the whole nation, the entire world had questions that weren't getting answered. The latest count had three local police officers, two county deputies, one civilian dispatcher, four young children, one service station operator, two sets of parents and the town manager either dead or missing, all under profoundly suspicious circumstances.

Cleary also came up with a famous mass murderer wearing Michelin tracks all over his mangled body.

Then throw in a tight-lipped police chief who'd seen what might or might not be the corpses of his two sons being bundled up and carted away by white-masked people flashing federal government identification cards.

All in all, you had a hell of a local event.

Laura May moved away from her front door and ducked the crack of daylight showing between her pulled drapes. Tom had advised her to stay away from prying eyes. Until things got sorted out in the next few days or months or—gods forbid—years, Tom told her it would be best to trust only him.

Everyone else was a potential enemy, most definitely including the Crockers and their brat and his little orphan buddy, Danny.

The widow returned to the back of her house, to where she'd been before Tom's interruption.

She had no better idea than anyone else as to what the hell had happened to her quiet town, to her quiet life. Without Tom Luckinbill's welcome assistance, the confusion and despair would have done her in. She had little doubt of that.

That's why she felt so defensive of him, why she ground her teeth in fury at every false or misleading story that appeared on the TV, the radio, in all the newspapers and news magazines and gossip rags. They all focused on the police chief's emotional withdrawal following the disappearances—or deaths, as the press incorrectly labeled them—of Greg and Tony. They questioned his unwillingness or inability to share what he knew in order to help them write rational stories and track unknown villains. Oh, how they would have loved to stick a camera in his face and watch the stern facade slide, like a snow-covered mountaintop, into an avalanche of despair.

They weren't going to see him come undone though, simply because he did know more than what he was telling.

"Don't listen to those others," her Vern told her once again as she took her customary seat in the room at the back of their house.

"Tom's doing just fine weathering the storm. Resting up, recovering from what these town bastards put him through. The Crocker kid, for instance, abandoning Greg and Tony like that. And let's not forget what his folks did to me when my back was turned. Then there's that bitch ex-wife of his, banging the new guy while still sharing poor Tom's bed, only to run off with the boys and try turning them against their own father. It just goes on and on, all the wrongs committed against that man."

Laura May, barely breathing, listened with a concentration level that imprinted her husband's every word in her mind. She wasted no time trying to reply. Communication was strictly one-sided for the time being, and could fade out without warning. But the signal did seem to be the slightest bit stronger today than the day before, or maybe that was just wishful thinking.

"Don't you be worrying, old girl. Our Tom's so much better for all of us than that psycho Durwood. Smart and sane, both. And boy does he have a score to settle. Me and Steve and Jeff and the others...we can't wait. There's gonna be a time coming soon enough, Laura May. I promise you that."

She sat in her favorite rocking chair, listening. She sat very still because she kept bumping into the bathtub and one of the sink legs every time she forgot about the cramped quarters and started to rock.

Laura May reached into the sink cabinet to rest the palm of one hand against the cool plumbing, as if she could coax more message from the throat of the bathroom fixture.

After a long moment she sighed. Experience taught her she'd have to wait patiently for the words to echo up to the surface and bob around the four surrounding walls. Sometimes her husband's nearly daily message came while she waited here in the bathroom, but more often he woke her in the middle of the night, which explained why she was always tired these days, always confused.

Laura May smiled. She knew how ludicrous she looked sitting here, drifting in and out of troubled sleep in the one room of the house that was never meant for sleep.

Nevertheless, Laura May sat very still and waited very quietly for further instructions from her husband and the others in the drains. She dreamed of that glorious day when she could see her Vern again, could hold him.

And when that day came, the world would know.

About the Author

David Searls is also the author of *Bloodthirst in Babylon* and *Malevolent*. He lives in the Cleveland, Ohio, area with his teenage son, Evan. Check out his blog at davidsearls.com.

Seize the day. Survive the night.

Bloodthirst in Babylon
© 2012 David Searls

They say if something looks too good to be true, it probably is. But folks across the country are desperate. Jobs are hard to find these days. So when the small town of Babylon offers work and even low rent at the local hotel, no one wants to look too closely. But they should. Babylon wants more than a workforce. Much more. There's something horrible behind the friendly smiles of the townspeople. Unfortunately, by the time the unlucky visitors realize that, it's too late. The trap has sprung. No one gets out of Babylon...alive.

Enjoy the following excerpt from Bloodthirst in Babylon...

The frozen-limbed mannequins still creeped Doyle out as he groped his way to the employees' exit, this time alone. He made it safely and turned to search the shadows for the on-duty manager who was supposed to lock up after him.

Doyle saw and heard no one, but he'd been told to leave, so he shrugged and stepped partially out of the doorway and peered at the parking lot. It stood nearly empty in the foggy yellow glow of a pair of tall sodium vapor lights. Past the lot, on Main View, traffic moved fairly steadily. It was a few minutes after nine, and dark.

"I want to get home before dark."

Now what the hell had the fool girl meant by that? Doyle pushed his way out and clanged the metal door closed behind him. His ears perked for even the smallest sounds. Habit, most likely, from the Badlands. He took a sharp right onto the pavement in front of the three-story building, then another onto the sidewalk of well-lit Main View Drive.

It was like day out here, people of all ages but mostly older, strolling and eating ice cream cones and walking dogs and gazing into lit store windows displaying shoes, hardware, rugs, books, banking and dry cleaning services, jewelry, food and coffee.

Nothing like his neighborhood, where folks really did need to get home before dark.

A car horn sounded and someone on the sidewalk playfully yelled at the driver.

Both sides of the street were lined with birch and maple saplings tethered to tree lawns to form skimpy green arches in front of the brick and wood-frame storefronts.

"...home before dark."

Funny, a young girl like that, afraid of walking alone with all these folks out on the streets.

"What a night."

The voice chilled him, nearly stopping him in his tracks. An old lady passed, dragging a yellow poodle that walked as though its feet hurt. Not her. The voice was young, insolent and male.

The blond-haired man came from nowhere to sidle up to Doyle. Said nothing now. Just smiled brightly in the streetlight.

He fell in and matched Doyle's pace. They wound their way through outdoor tables filled with ice-cream eaters and coffee sippers.

The street looked less well-lit the next block down.

The blond man snickered. He slowed, fell behind until Doyle couldn't see him without a glance over his shoulder. Jason Penney, in his early twenties, couldn't have gone more than one-fifty sopping wet. Doyle could take him easy if he had to—but where were Purcell and the others? He had to know.

An extended family out for a stroll made room for Doyle and the trailing Penney in front of a tire store still open for business. With the incandescent light leaking from a display window fully illuminating the scene for brief seconds, Doyle saw what looked to be four or five generations of a family, one member more wizened and slow-moving than the one before. Their lively chatter died as the two groups passed.

Penney laughed like he'd been expecting that reaction. "Finally some respect from this goddamn town," he said. He had a high, tight voice that would have seemed insolent just commenting on the weather.

Doyle said nothing. He watched a white-eyed figure on a painted bench. As he got closer, it became a slender, raven-haired young woman with a cigarette dangling between her lips. She caught his gaze.

"There you are," she said.

Huh?

She drew the cigarette from her lips, tapped out the ash on the ground and grinned as Doyle hurried on.

Another shadow, smaller than the girl, disengaged itself from a tree larger than the saplings in the previous block, and a boy in his early teens made Doyle veer. The boy snorted.

Footfalls. More pairs of feet than just Penney's following him like echoes. He forced himself to maintain a steady pace and not look back. He was nearly to Third Street. Half a block away, four elderly people sipped cool drinks at a café table set up in front of a bookstore. Three younger men drew around the seated figures and the four hurriedly rose and finished their drinks.

"Stay awhile, Grandma," one of the newcomers called out and the others hooted.

His deep rumble identified him immediately as the notorious Purcell.

Doyle had seen him with the cop, McConlon, on other nights. Just hanging, the two of them with heads together. Purcell's rigid face was now blue with stubble.

"How ya doing, Doyle?" Purcell said, eyes locked in on him as the old folks scuttled away.

Doyle wouldn't have even guessed that Purcell knew his name. *Bro;* that's all he'd heard from them before now.

"Hey, Duane, don't he look like the dude on TV?"

Coarse laughter. Lots of it.

Doyle whirled to see too many young men. They came closer, clustered around him in a claustrophobic circle. No, not just men. There was the slender dark-haired girl with the cigarette, and the younger boy. And still others coming at him from out of the darkness.

"You mean the comedian dude?" said Purcell. Then to Doyle: "Say something funny, bruthuh."

Doyle jerked backwards as something touched his foot. He looked down in disgust as he felt the rat's cold belly and sorry-assed tail slithering across his shoe and touching up against one bare ankle. He stepped back quickly as the thing ambled into the night.

"Jesus," he said.

The town was full of the things.

More wild laughter. Keep walking, he told himself. They wouldn't do anything with all these town folks out. Doyle had been stopped just out of the business district, and most of the strolling townspeople seemed to have found other placed to be, but he still saw the occasional car on the street out front and hand-holding couples quickly squeezing past the crowd on the sidewalk. It was too busy out here for him to be in any real danger.

Besides, The Sundown was just a couple more blocks to the east. Not far at all in a car. Course, he was on foot. And currently surrounded by eight or ten townies who didn't look like they were there to safeguard his way back.

Purcell broke from the circle and sat at the outdoor table the two elderly couples had hurriedly vacated. He made a quick hand motion and someone from the back of the cluster dropped something heavy onto the tabletop. He grunted at the effort and the glass-topped table shuddered.

Doyle swallowed to wet the cement that had formed in his throat. "Okay, a suitcase," he said, trying to keep it light.

Yeah, a scuffed leather suitcase that—

"Hey," he said in the next moment. "That's mine!"

Something squealed as more fat, long-tailed bodies rolled across his feet. Doyle tried to back up, but he'd run out of space. He could feel hot breath huffing down his neck, and smelled the strong scent of rancid meat.

"What the hell?" he snapped, anger momentarily overruling fear.

He moved in to snatch the suitcase—*his* luggage—but Purcell swatted it off the table. It fell heavily and someone scooped it up and made it disappear in the crowd.

Something about the feeble streetlight out front made Purcell's eyes shine white-hot.

"How did you...?"

Doyle's anger had already started to turn to leaden dread as he considered what it meant that Purcell had his things. First, that they'd broken into his room at The Sundown, and had obviously packed his bag. Where was Carl during all this? Had they hurt him?

He could hear the sound of a zipper unzipping, and then the slender-haired girl said, "Check this out."

She'd opened his suitcase and now held up a pair of his wildly patterned undershorts, drawing hoots of laughter.

Catching quick peeks at the street, Doyle could see a few cars cruising by without slowing to investigate the sidewalk mob. Maybe even speeding up.

"So now you're all packed up with nowhere to go," said Purcell, still seated.

"You broke into my place."

"Not me," said Purcell. "Friend of mine, this afternoon. And he didn't break in. He used a key. Left the place looking as neat and tidy as he found it."

Doyle's fury got him moving. He wheeled and headed straight for the nearest body, determined to steamroll through it if he had to. But he didn't. The crowd unexpectedly parted. That's all they wanted to do, just tease him. Freak him out, scare the scary black man away.

Their plan had worked to perfection. He wouldn't even go through the motions of filing a police report. Let them keep his underwear and toothbrush and ragged suitcase. Small price to pay. He'd be out of there by morning. Carl could tag along if he wanted. Or stay. That was fine, too.

It took a few seconds for Doyle to realize he was leading a crowd. He heard Penney giggling behind him and a few others muttering, but they kept their distance. Kept it until they drew even with a parking lot fronting a florist shop with three customers chatting away on the other side of an inviting expanse of warmly lit display glass.

As they closed in, Doyle threw his elbow back and connected with Jason Penney's throat. He enjoyed the hell out of hearing the townie gagging and puking, but everything went very bad very quickly after that.

As they fell on him, Doyle's first thought was that this was going to be the worst beating of his life. But that was interrupted by other thoughts, much darker ones, when the first set of teeth nestled deep into his groin.

Available now in ebook and print from Samhain Publishing.

THE BEST IN HORROR

Every month Samhain brings you the finest in horror fiction from the most respected names in the genre, as well as the most talented newcomers. From subtle chills to shocking terror, experience the ultimate in fear from such brilliant authors as:

Ramsey Campbell   W. D. Gagliani

Ronald Malfi   Greg F. Gifune

Brian Moreland   John Everson

And many more!

THE HOUSE OF HORROR

Samhain Horror books are available at your local bookstore, or you can check out our Web site, www.samhainhorror.com, where you can look up your favorite authors, read excerpts and see upcoming releases.

PUBLISHING

It's all about the story...

Romance

HORROR

www.samhainpublishing.com

CPSIA information can be obtained at www.ICGtesting.com
Printed in the USA
LVOW11s1920160214

373901LV00005B/1059/P